CLEAVER
&COMPANY

BY JAMES DUFFY

CLEAVER
& COMPANY

James Duffy

CHARLES SCRIBNER'S SONS · NEW YORK
Maxwell Macmillan Canada · Toronto
Maxwell Macmillan International
New York · Oxford · Singapore · Sydney

This novel is a work of fiction. Names, characters, places, and incidents are either the product of the author's imagination or are used fictitiously. Any resemblance to actual persons living or dead, events, or locales is entirely coincidental.

Charles Scribner's Sons Books for Young Readers
Macmillan Publishing Company
866 Third Avenue, New York, NY 10022

Maxwell Macmillan Canada, Inc.
1200 Eglinton Avenue East, Suite 200
Don Mills, Ontario M3C 3N1

Macmillan Publishing Company is part of the
Maxwell Communication Group of Companies.

First Edition   10 9 8 7 6 5 4 3 2 1
Printed in the United States of America

Library of Congress Cataloging-in-Publication Data
Duffy, James, date.
  Cleaver & company / James Duffy. — 1st ed.   p.   cm.
  Summary: The summer she turns thirteen, Sarah is kept busy working in her family's diner and dealing with their big dog Cleaver. Sequel to "Cleaver of the Good Luck Diner."
  ISBN 0-684-19371-X
  [1. Dogs—Fiction. 2. Restaurants, lunch rooms, etc.—Fiction. 3. Family life—Fiction.] I. Title. II. Title: Cleaver and company.
PZ7.D87814Ck 1991   [Fic]—dc20   91-9932

For S.Z.H.D.

CLEAVER
&COMPANY

—*1*—

Mom took the truck driver's pie plate and cup and saucer, scraped the twenty-five-cent tip into Cori's cigar box, and went into the kitchen. From under the table in booth number four Cleaver lifted his head to see if a bit of crust had fallen under the counter stool. Disappointed, he sighed and put his head down between his paws.

"Want a soft drink, Sarah?" Mom shouted.

"No, thanks. I'm on a diet, remember?" I stretched out on the backseat of booth number four. I kicked off my loafers and buried my feet in Cleaver's fur. He was shedding all over the place, and Mom was starting to mutter about tying him to the maple tree in back. Outside, the parking lot was empty. There wasn't much traffic in the early afternoons. Later, the computer factory would let out, and we'd have some early supper business. Not much, though. On Fridays most people went straight home.

"A diet drink?" Mom called.

1

"No, thanks."

"Anything else, a carrot or a slice of cold meat loaf?"

"No, thanks."

"Why don't you take Cleaver to the playing field while it's quiet here? Maybe one of your friends will be there. Just be back by four. I don't think Dad is going to make it this afternoon."

"There's no one there the first couple of weeks after school lets out, except for Little League practice. Besides, since Cleaver got his limp he doesn't like to walk much."

Mom slumped on the bench across from me. She stirred some sugar into her coffee. "It's not much of a beginning to summer, is it? Well, it will straighten around, just wait and see. Maybe they'll put the new road in, tear down our diner, and we won't have to worry anymore. Won't that be the day?"

About a month ago a survey gang had gone to work on the road. They were out there a couple of days with stakes and lines and poles, shouting back and forth. Mom sent Cori to see what was going on. When Cori came back with the message they were surveying for a new road, Mom decided to find out for herself. She came back pale and upset. "It's for a cutoff to the interstate. Right down between the diner and the rest home. They might have to take the parking lot and the diner."

Dad talked to the town engineer, who said not to worry, it was just a survey to keep on file. But Mom didn't believe that for a minute. There had been a lot of talk for a couple of years about connecting Stanhope with the interstate highway to bring more business into town.

Everything was going wrong at once. Even before school let out, I could feel it building. Things should have been better because Dad was back living with us now, but he hadn't been home a month before he and Mom were arguing again. Dad had started out with lots of promises when he came back, but he didn't keep them very long. He was still bored with life in the diner. "I'm fed up, Nettie," he complained, when Mom reminded him of his promise to help out in the diner three late afternoons and evenings a week. "Let's sell the place and give everyone a break. It's wearing all of us out. I'm doing pretty well in the launderette business. I've put a batch of machines in at the college that will bring in a lot. No rent, no water bill—it's a good deal. The kids kept breaking the ones the school put in."

"What's to keep them from tearing yours up, too, Ed?" Mom wanted to know.

"I'm buying a new machine the Germans make, a heavy-duty. An elephant couldn't hurt it. What do you say, Nettie? Let's sell. Give yourself and the girls a rest. I'll look after you all."

I remembered every word Mom said in a real serious voice. It was after closing time last Saturday night—one of Dad's agreed-on nights—and he was sweating and complaining. Mom turned around, angrier even than when Dad had taken it into his head to leave home the year before.

"It's *my* place, Ed. Remember? Mama and I bought your half with our own good money. There's not a penny of Stuart money in the Good Luck Diner. It kept the kids and Mama and me going while you were off trying to figure out what life was all about, and it will have to keep us again when you take off the next time. I can see that's on your mind already. I couldn't care less whether you pitch in here or not—helping out was your idea—but we all care that you stay with us. We care more than you seem to understand. I'm not going to depend on you to look after us, though. Not now or ever. If they put the road in, we'll move the diner somewhere else."

Dad kept getting redder as Mom lit into him. He shuffled around in the kitchen and pretended he was interested in being sure the dishwasher was working the way it should. Cleaver had padded out to the kitchen to see what the noise was. When he saw what was going on, he put his tail down and went back underneath the table at booth number four. He wasn't around to see Dad come up to Mom with an embarrassed smile and wrap his arms around her in apology. "Let's go look at the ten o'clock movie, Nettie. We'll work it out."

When the lights went out in the front of the diner, Cleaver came to the back door, ears and tail up, ready to go up to the house. He danced around Mom and put his paws on her shoulder to lick her face. He nuzzled Dad a

4

couple of times to tell him everything was all right. Cleaver didn't like arguments and loud talk. He was a very orderly dog most of the time and liked to have things go on smoothly around him. "Look at him," Granny Rubin said sometimes when Cleaver was being very serious. "He thinks he's a Swiss banker, not a deli dog. Isn't that so, big boy?" Then she would hold out a scrap of something good she had put aside for him.

Now Cleaver was under my feet, panting like crazy in the afternoon heat, waiting for someone to come in and drop a crumb on the floor. Mom reached down for a second to scratch him behind his ears. "You don't like the heat, do you, baby? Just you wait; if it stays like this, I'll turn the air conditioner on. It's an awful expense. I keep hoping it will turn cool again."

"It's almost July, Mom. It's going to stay hot now. I'll need it, too, you know, if I'm going to fill in for Linda."

That was another thing. Just before the year ended at the college, Linda Kowelski, who worked in the diner from noon to closing time, landed a job in a summer camp teaching kids who were a little slow. That was her specialty in the education program at the college. Mom told Linda to take the job. She said summers weren't so busy and Dad and I could fill in until August, when she would close down for a month. Cori and I would go to Maine and she and Dad would take a break somewhere special. That was before Dad stopped helping out the way he said he would, and now Mom wasn't even sure she and Dad would be taking a vacation together.

Mom didn't say anything about Cori's helping out. Cori used to clean off the counters in the evenings, but these days it seemed she only came home to sleep. She spent the rest of the time down the road with her *very* best friend, Margo Michaels. As soon as she finished breakfast she was out the door. "See you later," she'd yell over her shoulder. Part of it was not to have to listen to Mom and Dad fussing. It upset Cori more than it did me. "I can't take it, Sarah," she whispered when I went into her room for our good-night talk. "It was better before Dad came back home. We had Mom and Granny Rubin and it was nice and quiet. Dad doesn't want to be here."

I realized Mom was talking to me. "What do you think I ought to do, Sarah, close up for the summer? We'd lose all our steadies. But it will be hard without Cori and Linda, and I just don't feel like training anybody else. I was counting on your father. It was a mistake for him to come back, wasn't it? First he got tired of the diner and now I can see he's getting tired of the laundry business. He's put those machines in at the college so he won't have to be here and because he can say later that the launderettes were too much for him and he's going to do something else. I don't know what he's trying to prove."

Cleaver whined for me to rub his back. "Maybe he could breed dogs, Mom. He's awfully good with them. We could have a kennel in the barn if Dad fixed the roof." I liked the thought of little Cleavers running around up the hill. "Bernese mountain dogs cost a lot of money these days, he says."

Mom sniffed. "And who would look after them when your father got tired of the dog business? No, thank you. One Cleaver is enough. One lame, overweight Cleaver is quite enough for all of us."

—2—

No one had come into the diner since the truck driver left an hour ago. Cleaver crawled out from under the table. His food clock told him it was four o'clock, time for his afternoon banana ice cream. Cori wasn't there to scoop it out, so he sat down and rested his head on the end of the table, not panting for a moment, and waited. When nothing happened, he barked once to let us know what time it was. Mom reached out to scratch the white spot on top of his head. When she stopped, Cleaver barked twice and went to the freezer behind the counter. I guess he still expected Cori to show up. He sounded anxious, the way he always did when things didn't go on schedule. "That dog has a Swiss watch in his head," Granny Rubin said. "We don't even have to wind it up."

"We need to give him something, Mom. You can't stop feeding him because he's put on some weight. You just offered me a soft drink, and I'm on a diet, too."

"It was a diet root beer, Sarah, not a bowl of ice cream."

"I don't care. The poor dog has to have something. He can't go all day on his breakfast." I got up and slouched out to the kitchen. Cleaver limped after me. He sat patiently while I poked around in the refrigerator. I pinched off a section of cold meat loaf and held it down for him. Cleaver sniffed it politely before he took it. Then he gulped it down without chewing. He looked up for more.

"That's it, Cleaver. You're getting as fat as I am." In the kitchen heat, I realized I felt really heavy. Mom said it was developmental, whatever that meant. She told me she was tubby until she went off to college. Granny Rubin, who was listening, said Mom was only plump, just right to please the boys—which made Mom mad. "I was overweight, Mama, because you stuffed me like a goose."

The kids at school said I was fat, too, not plump or tubby or developmental, but fat. Even Mrs. Porter commented toward the end of the year on how I looked. "You're putting on weight these days, aren't you, Sarah? Too much of your mother's cooking, I bet. Just remember those pounds are harder to take off than they are to put on."

That was the way it was with Mrs. Porter: She was straightforward with her students. I didn't mind too much, but I figured it wasn't any of her business to talk about my weight when she asked me to drop by after school.

"Your grades are falling off again, Sarah, and you

9

aren't writing for me—not anything very good, that is. The last couple of stories weren't half as good as you can do. You're holding back, avoiding those things that you used to write about—you know, like your family and Cleaver and what you think about growing up. Is something wrong? Your father's home now, isn't he? Has that made a difference?"

When I didn't answer, Mrs. Porter saw that she had asked the wrong question. "Well, I just wanted to talk to you before school was over. We haven't seen much of each other lately. Try to have a good summer. You're going to Maine, aren't you? That should be a nice change. And bring me some writing in September. Keep at it, Sarah. I'm confident I'm going to see your name on a book jacket someday." Mrs. Porter stood up and stuck out her hand, and that was that. Somehow I felt even fatter and more useless.

That was something else that worried Mom—my grades. She shook her head when she saw an almost solid row of C's on my final report card. Mrs. Porter gave me a B in English, and the domestic-science teacher gave me a B because she liked to eat at the Good Luck. "I don't know about high school, Sarah," Mom said. "They say Stanhope High isn't much good now. They've lost a lot of teachers and had to cut back on the academic programs. I don't know. We might have to look into the private schools."

That meant St. Eulalia's, the girls' Catholic school. "No way, Mom. I'm not going to wear a uniform for four years."

10

"It's not a uniform. It's a pleated skirt and a blazer. They look better than those acid jeans you wear," Mom said.

I snitched another pinch of meat loaf for Cleaver. "Do you want to go for a walk, Cleaver? Go get your leash." Cleaver ignored me. He turned around and went back to his place under the table.

"What are we going to do about him?" Mom asked. "He waddles, he's so big. It looks like his limp is worse. What did the doctor say the last time you and Dad took him in?"

"He said he didn't know what was wrong, but it might work itself out. He also said Cleaver was carrying too much weight. The funny thing is that it's not the back leg where he put the pin in Cleaver's hip. That's fine. It's the front leg he's limping on. Dr. Fuller says that some dogs compensate for injuries and maybe Cleaver is walking different because of his broken hip. Also he has a cyst on his front paw, but that doesn't seem to be the cause, either."

"Can't he take an X ray or something? It doesn't seem right the poor dog should go through life limping."

"He'll have to knock Cleaver out to take an X ray. He's not ready to do that. Put him on a diet, he said. I felt for a minute like he was talking about me. He looked up at me and smiled, not saying anything, but you could see he wanted to say, 'You, too.'"

"You mustn't be so sensitive, Sarah. And don't listen to your friends. Most of the girls are just like you."

"It's not so, Mom. No one except Stacy Wilcox and

that's because both her mother and father are huge. How many seventh graders do you see who weigh a hundred and forty pounds? Not even the boys. I've put on twenty pounds in the last three months. I don't understand it, Mom. I feel like eating all the time."

"Since Dad came back, and we fuss and fight all the time? It's made you and Cleaver anxious, hasn't it? Dogs are sensitive, too."

It was true. I *was* anxious. And I could see that Cleaver was worrying about things. Cori had run away, down the road to Margo Michaels. But there was no place for me to go. I couldn't tell Mom that, so I said, "I don't think so, Mom. It must be developmental, just the way you said."

Mom was looking out the window at the parking lot shimmering in the heat. "I don't know about Dad, honestly. It's not that we don't want to be together or don't love each other. It seems to me we can't agree on anything. I learned a lot, Sarah, while Dad was gone. Mostly I learned I could look after the diner and my family without any help. I want Dad's respect, and we'll get along fine. When he and I take our vacation in August, we'll see if we can work things out. I'll keep my word to go off for a month. Afterward we'll see. Maine will be good for you girls and Cleaver, too. If he goes swimming every day, he'll lose some weight."

3

At five o'clock cars began to pour into the parking lot.
Right then Dad called up from the college. The new
German washing machines weren't working out the way
he predicted. The summer-school kids had jammed
them with foreign coins. Mom was really mad now. "Go
get Granny Rubin, Sarah. She'll have to take over the
register." She flipped the air conditioner on.

"I can do the register, Mom. I've done it before." The
register was the best part of working in the diner. It was
an old Burroughs register that my grandfather had
found in a junk shop about the time he opened the Good
Luck Diner. He and Dad had fixed it up and polished
it. The register had silver scrolls at the top and a bell
that rang when you opened it—to keep the help from
stealing, Granny Rubin said—and a little marble shelf
over the cash drawer. Mom had lots of offers from people who wanted to buy or trade their computer registers
for it. "I can't part with it," she used to say. "It's part of

the diner." Mom promised I could mind the register next fall when I fill in for Linda or Granny Rubin.

"And take Cleaver with you," Mom ordered. "He'll be in the way out here now." When the diner had begun to fill up, Cleaver had slouched out to the kitchen and curled up in a tight little ball under the worktable. He was too big now to stretch out under the plate shelf behind the counter. He didn't really get in Mom's way, except when something dropped from the table. Then Cleaver stuck his big head out to snap it up; Mom was afraid she'd trip over him or drop something hot on him.

"Come on, Cleaver," I said. "Come on quick!"

Cleaver looked up, ears back and tail wagging, which was his way of telling me he was getting along fine where he was and had no intention of moving.

"Cleaver!" Mom said, exasperated. "Can't you ever do anything right? Let him be. Call Granny Rubin on the phone. And look after the people in booths two and three. They've been here for a while. Scoot."

"I'm still in my housecoat, Sarah. Why didn't you call earlier?" Granny Rubin said. "What's with your mother? 'Fridays are dull. We don't need you tonight,' she said. Now she needs me. I'll be down as soon as I can."

"Granny Rubin will be here as soon as she can," I called into the kitchen, and ran to booth two. "Sorry to keep you waiting. We usually don't have much business on Fridays. My mother gave the waitress the day off."

"That's okay," the woman said, looking at the menu.

"It's too hot to cook. The boys here want cheeseburgers and french fries and ginger ale, I guess. I'll take the garden salad. What are you having, Phil?"

"A steak, rare, and fries. You don't sell beer, eh?"

"No, sir."

"Just water, then. And a small salad."

I slipped the order on the counter to the kitchen and dashed to the third booth. The people there were an old couple, and they were upset. The woman had her lips set to give me a scolding, and the man was puffing himself up to tell me something important. "We were here before the people in the other booth," the woman said.

"I'm sorry, ma'am. Their kids were impatient. We're having problems this evening."

"I can see that," the man said. "It looks like you're part of the problem."

I didn't answer that. "Would you like to order?"

"I don't think we should stay if you can't take care of your customers in order. Do you, Miller?"

Now her husband made a big show of looking at his watch. "We're going to be late for the first show. No point in waiting. We wouldn't even make the second show, probably, if we were to eat here."

"If you give me your order, we'll hurry it up for you," I urged.

The woman stood. "You'll have to look after those other folks first," she said in a nasty voice. She and Miller moved out.

15

"What's with them?" Mom asked. "Tired of waiting?"

"I'm sorry."

"It's not your fault. We get all kinds."

By the time Granny Rubin made her way down the hill, the rush had died out. "So what's the big hurry, Benedicta? Where's your husband? You don't need me on Ed's night, you said. So where is Ed?"

"Fixing some broken washing machines."

In the kitchen Cleaver heard Granny Rubin talking and came out to greet her. On his way Cleaver reached up to grab a dish towel. That was his way of greeting family who came into the diner or the house. It didn't have to be a dish towel; it could be a shoe or jacket or sweater, practically anything except the plastic bone he was supposed to use. He held on to whatever he had in his mouth and growled when you tried to get it from him. You had to give him a big hug or a snack, either one, before he'd drop the towel.

Granny reached in her pocket for a dried prune, which was his diet snack now that he didn't get a bowl of ice cream. He was big on prunes, especially the pitted ones. He'd eat ones with pits, but if he smelled the pit, he'd gulp it down without chewing. The others, he liked to chew a couple of times to get the flavor.

Off and on until closing time, groups of customers kept coming in. I wasn't as good a waitress as Linda Kowelski—Linda was a real pro, Mom said—but I was learning fast. I got a couple of orders mixed up, but

16

people were very nice about it, especially when they found out my mother ran the diner. It turned out most of the people didn't come from Stanhope. There had been an article on diners in the Hartford paper, which most everybody took, and there was a picture of the Good Luck Diner. It was the first hot weekend of the year, and people out on a drive had come to Stanhope to eat in a real old-fashioned diner.

I couldn't keep track of the tips, I was so busy. There were lots of dollar bills. I dumped them all into the cigar box Cori said was hers. Cori was the one who counted the money and put the figure in a little black accounts book before Mom took it off to the bank for us. Up to now most of the tips were Cori's—change she picked up from an ice-cream customer or coins Linda gave her for helping out when things got tight.

Now that I was working full-time, I asked Mom if I shouldn't have my tips in my account. That made Cori howl, because she had to share her tips fifty-fifty with me. Mom said we shouldn't get into fights about who did what. All the money went into a single college account. Some days it would be Cori who earned more and other days it would be me. That's the way it was.

In the meantime Mom intended to pay me a salary, which I could either keep in my room or put in the bank, just as I chose. "I'll pay you, too," she said to Cori, "if you decide to work in the diner instead of down at Mr. Michaels's."

"No way," Cori said. "I'm going to be a farmer when I grow up. I'm learning how now."

Mom started to answer back, but she didn't. I could see what she wanted to say. She wanted to say it was about time for Cori to grow up and help out at home. But Cori was still her baby, and Mom didn't want her to grow up too fast. Only me.

A little after nine when the last customer had left, Mom locked the front door to the parking lot, flicked off the sign, and told me to leave the pots and pans until tomorrow. I turned on the dishwasher. I was exhausted.

Mom was waiting at the back door. "Maybe we can persuade Dad to clean up tomorrow. The floor needs a good scrubbing, and the windows are filthy." The Good Luck wasn't open on Sundays. Usually Mom and Cori and I cleaned the place up for a couple of hours in the afternoon so it would be spic and span when we opened up at six o'clock Monday morning for the truckers and delivery people.

Cleaver squeezed out the screen door the second Mom undid the latch. He thumped up the path to the house as fast as he could go. He looked like a small elephant disappearing in the dark.

"Funny thing about Cleaver's limp," Mom commented. "When he's in a hurry it seems to disappear. Isn't that so?"

"Yeah," I said. "I noticed that, too. When I drag him to the playing field, he limps like he can't take another step. And soon as he's off his leash, he runs around like a puppy. I told the vet. All he said was it happens like that sometimes."

"I think Cleaver's bum leg is in his head," Mom said. "He must be compensating for his diet, not his broken hip. He's discovered Granny slips him a snack when he limps up to her and puts his head in her lap. Cleaver's a tramp."

We were halfway up the hill when Dad's Winnebago swung into the driveway. He touched the horn and blinked his lights as he went past. He hopped out of the cab and was waiting at the kitchen door with a hug and a kiss for Mom. She pushed on past, in no mood to be friendly. Dad went into a long explanation about the jammed coin slots on the washing machines. "So what else is new, Ed?" Mom said.

Dad didn't answer. He put his head down and let Cleaver out.

"That dog is no good," Granny Rubin was muttering. "In the house one minute and yelping to get out the next."

"After he got his snack, I bet," Mom said. "He's too fat, Mama. Lay off the snacks."

"Cleaver's still a growing boy. It was nothing much, Benedicta. Only a little bit of crust I had left over from the apple pie. I baked it along with the pie. Cleaver does like his crust."

"Why shouldn't he? It's 110 percent fat," Mom replied.

Every night as soon as we turned off the lights in the diner, Cleaver waited at the door to run up the hill for his snack from Granny Rubin, who left at eight or eight-thirty unless it was busy right up until nine. Then Cleaver had to go right back outside to see if Cori was on her way home from the Michaelses'. He ran across the field to the sit-down place to wait.

Cori usually came along a minute or two later. She was supposed to leave Margo's at nine on the dot, but, Cori being Cori, she had to push it to five after, even a few minutes beyond that. She had turned ten in May and was feeling grown-up. When Mom told her again nine o'clock exactly, Cori answered that she was training Cleaver to be patient and she had to give him time to get to the sit-down place. Once she had him trained, she'd leave at nine on the dot.

The sit-down place was halfway across the slope between our barn and the Michaelses' truck garden. Mr. Michaels drove a school bus during the season and had a four-acre truck garden he cultivated in the summer. He had a vegetable stand beside the road where he sold produce, starting with lettuce in the early spring and on to pumpkins in the fall. Mrs. Michaels grew flowers she sold at the stand along with eggs her hens laid and home-made jelly and pies. This year Mr. Michaels intended to sell homemade ice cream and lemonade. He put Margo and her best friend ever, Cori, in charge of that part of the operation.

First, the two of them had to help plant the garden. Kids' fingers were better than big fingers for putting tiny lettuce and carrot seeds in the ground, Mr. Michaels said. And for pulling out the early weeds. So he hired Cori to help out six weeks before school ended. That was practically the last we saw of her.

Cleaver belonged to Cori more than to anyone else, so he went along once in a while to keep track of her. He was welcome, Mr. Michaels said, as long as he stayed out of the garden. "I have enough troubles with ground-hogs and crows and rabbits and even a deer or two," he told Cleaver. "I don't need a Bernese in my garden."

Cleaver paid attention for a couple of days. Then he got bored and one hot day dug himself a nice cool hole to rest in—right in the middle of the lettuce patch. He was banished from the truck garden, so Cori was training him to wait for her on the hillside. It didn't take her long. A little something in her pocket was all she needed. Cleaver gobbled Granny Rubin's snack and bounded out the door to collect Cori's.

At nine-thirty when Cori hadn't shown up, Granny Rubin began to fret. Dad and I were watching television. Upstairs Mom was washing the grease and smoke out of her hair. At nine-forty Granny Rubin poked her head out the door to listen. "I don't hear them," she reported. "Go see where they are, Sarah."

22

"She's just late again," I argued. "Wait a few minutes." When the commercial break came, Granny was at my side to shoo me outside. She had read in the paper that someone had sighted a bear in the state park north of Stanhope, and she was certain that it was waiting to grab Cori. Cleaver had daily instructions from Granny Rubin to watch out for the bear.

Outside I listened. You could usually hear Cori and Cleaver as they made their way home from the sit-down place. Tonight I didn't hear anything. I wanted to go inside to see the end of the program. "Cori," I shouted. "Here, Cleaver. Come on. Hurry up." I barked a couple of times. That usually caught Cleaver's attention. Silence. I waited, listening hard. A falling star flashed across the sky. I made a wish for myself and went back inside to see the program.

Mom was drying her hair in the kitchen. "First I lose my husband," she said in a voice for Dad to hear. "Now I've lost my daughter. Call up Margo, Sarah, and have her send Cori home on the double."

Margo wasn't to be seen. Mrs. Michaels made me wait while she called upstairs and outside. "Goodness," she reported. "I don't know where they are. Harry and I were watching that new show, and I wasn't paying attention. I thought Cori had left and Margo was in her room. We'll take a look outside."

I had missed the last part of the new show. I reported to Granny Rubin that Mrs. Michaels was sending Cori home as soon as she found her. That wasn't good enough for her. "It's the bear," she decided. "He's got both of them and Cleaver, too. It's a grizzly, not one of those little black bears. I read that out west . . ."

"Oh, Mama," Mom said. "Ed, will you and Sarah take a walk down to the Michaelses' to meet her?"

Cleaver was waiting patiently at the sit-down place. You couldn't tell in the dark, but I think he looked anxious. He turned to greet Dad and me and kept on looking and sniffing down the path. Dad slipped the leash on Cleaver and he lunged ahead of us.

"Hi, Ed. You here, too, are you, Sarah?" Mr. Michaels said. "Isn't this the darndest thing?" He flashed his big flashlight across the garden. "They stayed outside trying to catch a few lightning bugs that came out early because of the heat. I went inside to clean up. Sometime between eight-thirty and nine. They must be around here somewhere, but I'll be darned if I know where. They didn't answer. Let's see if that fancy dog of yours can help. He looks like he has some bloodhound in him."

"Cleaver." I leaned down to explain. "Cleaver, where's Cori? And Margo? Go find them, Cleaver. Find Cori."

"Don't let him off the leash, Sarah," Mr. Michaels said. "The garden is all planted now."

Cleaver looked up at me. He whined and sat down.

"Let's take him into the field, Sarah," Dad said. "He's a field dog, not a garden dog. His relatives look after sheep in Switzerland."

"Cori isn't a sheep, Dad. He doesn't understand." I led Cleaver into the meadow in back of the truck garden. You could just see the outline of the woods which ran across the ridge all the way to the state park. It was scary. Maybe the bear had come out of the woods. "Have you seen the bear around here?" I asked Mr. Michaels.

"That old bear?" he laughed. "People have been seeing that bear since I was a boy. There's no bear in the woods, that's just talk. Why, look at Cleaver. He's pulling hard. Turn him loose now."

Cleaver tore through the grass up the hillside. He paused for a moment to see if we were following. He wasn't sniffing the ground the way I had seen bloodhounds on television do. Head high, Cleaver was charging straight through the grass.

"Now, I know where they're at," Mr. Michaels said. "They're playing in the old Cotter shed. They've been up there a couple of times. I used to play up there myself. The old place is still dry inside. Margo!" he shouted. He flashed his light ahead of him. It reflected on a window pane.

Mr. Michaels stood in the doorway with his light. There were two sleeping bags on the floor. Margo and Cori had burrowed inside. Cleaver had his head inside Cori's bag. He pulled it back out chewing.

"We're having a sleep-over, Dad," Margo said. "We left a note on the kitchen table. Mom was supposed to call Cori's mother."

"Well, we didn't see it. You're too young to sleep up here by yourselves. There's a bear in those woods. Maybe next year if Sarah and the dog here come along, too. Good dog, Cleaver. You knew where they were, didn't you?"

Cleaver wasn't paying attention to Mr. Michaels. He waited until Cori climbed out of the sleeping bag, then sniffed at her pocket.

"He knew where we were," she said. "Didn't you, Cleaver?" She handed Cleaver another prune.

Cleaver sniffed to see if it had a pit. Then he chewed it a couple of times before he swallowed.

—5—

"You two hold the fort," Mom said to Granny Rubin and me. "I have to go over to Madison to the wholesale-supply place. Ed promised to pick the stuff up when he went there yesterday, but . . ." Her voice trailed off. The evening before when Dad came back without the supplies for the shelf and freezer, Mom had given him some harsh words and told him to go on up to the house and watch television, he wasn't any use to her.

"Ed has a lot on his mind, Benedicta," Granny Rubin said. "He forgot, that's all. People forget things."

"How come you never forget to stick up for Ed, Mama? I'll be back by five—unless I forget."

Granny Rubin and I were playing checkers at booth four. It was still hot, and the air conditioner was rattling away over the back door. Dad had promised to tighten it up, but he hadn't gotten around to that, either.

"Where's your dog, Sarah?" Granny asked. "I have room for my feet under the table for a change. Did he run down to the Michaelses'?"

"He's in the kitchen under the work table. He's moved out there. Mom says he stays there to aggravate her. He doesn't like to move much in the summer. The first place he flops down he stays. Now he does his first flopping in the kitchen. He's losing weight. He doesn't shake so much when he walks."

"It's the prunes," Granny Rubin declared. "I knew they'd do the trick."

Actually, I was the one who had started on the prunes for my own weight problem, then I started sharing them with Cleaver, but I didn't say anything.

"I'm worried about Benedicta," Granny Rubin said, double jumping two of my checkers into the corner of the board. "King me."

I had only two checkers left. It was the third straight game I had lost. I dumped the checkers into their box and folded up the board. The week before Granny Rubin and I had played poker in slack time. Granny Rubin was good at poker, too.

"You have to pay attention when you play games, Sarah. I'm worried about you, too."

I waited a while before I answered. I wasn't ready for another lecture on my weight. "What about?" I finally asked.

"You're growing up like your mother. She was always a worrier. Even before she was twelve, like you, she worried about things."

"I'm thirteen, Granny Rubin, remember? June 6, that was my birthday."

"No matter. Twelve or thirteen, you're a worrier. I was never a worrier, even when your grandfather and I had to leave Germany in a hurry. I came here. I let him do the worrying."

I wondered what Granny Rubin was trying to tell me. I didn't remember my grandfather all that well, but it seemed to me he was always pretty happy about things.

Granny Rubin had a faraway look in her eyes. "Abram," she said, "he was the serious one. Like Benedicta. I always went along with whatever Abram said."

"You mean Mom should do what Dad says, or wants to do, is that it, Granny Rubin?" I asked.

"I didn't say that, Sarah."

If I were a worrier like Mom, what did that make Cori? "What about Cori?" I asked. "Is she a worrier?"

Granny Rubin smiled. Cori was her baby. "Of course not, she's too young to worry. She's just a little girl. Cori's like me—and your father. She looks more like Ed. You look like your mother, Sarah, kind of serious and plump."

Thanks a lot, Granny Rubin, I thought. Maybe I could have Cleaver on my side. "What about Cleaver?"

Granny Rubin gave Cleaver some thought. "Well, I can't say yet. He had an unhappy childhood."

I hadn't heard about Cleaver's unhappy childhood. He certainly wasn't unhappy after he came to live with us, growing up on banana ice cream and Mom's meat loaf. "What do you mean? I don't think he has any problems."

"Your dad told me that Cleaver was the runt of the litter. His mother couldn't feed him and kicked him out of the puppy box. He was an orphan, which is why Ed chose him." Granny Rubin sniffed at the thought of Cleaver being an orphan. She took a prune from her apron pocket and called Cleaver in from the kitchen. He settled under the table, keeping an eye out for customers. "Cleaver is his own dog, I think," Granny Rubin decided.

That left only Dad, who could do no wrong in Granny Rubin's eyes, even after he walked out on us a year or so ago. "And Dad?" I asked. "Granny Stuart is very serious. So was Dr. Stuart, I bet."

"Your father has learned to enjoy life, Sarah. He doesn't worry about things. That's the way to be. You and your mother should learn to enjoy life. Like the rest of us. Right, Cleaver?"

It was a good thing Mom wasn't there to hear what Granny Rubin was saying. The older she got, the more Granny Rubin wanted to have her own way about how things were. Mom had her own opinions about how things were, especially Dad's ways. "It's enough I have to fight with Ed, Mama," she'd say, "without you pitching in to take his side." When she said that, Cori and I tried to disappear, because Granny Rubin always said that Ed was the best husband any woman could ask for and then Mom really got started.

I looked out the window where the heat was bouncing off the asphalt. A black car, maybe a Ford, pulled slowly into the parking lot. It parked in the far corner, which was sort of stupid because the guy could have parked right alongside the diner. He sat in the car for a while; he appeared to be looking at something in his lap.

Then he got out and stood beside the car studying the Good Luck Diner. He was a short man with glasses

31

and wore a hat, one of those lightweight straw ones, sitting square on top of his head. And a dark suit. He looked cool and official. I suddenly had a feeling in my bones. At that moment I would have bet a million dollars the man was the health inspector. I reached under the table. "Come on, Cleaver," I ordered. "Time to get out of here."

Cleaver lifted his brown eyebrows to tell me sadly but firmly he didn't want to move. I grabbed his collar. Cleaver went limp. When I loosened my grip he rolled over on his back and put his paws up to push me away. Where was the leash? I'd have to drag him outside. It was up in the house, I remembered. I had seen it there on the chair by the door when I came down the hall.

"Come on, Cleaver," I screamed. "Out!" I held the back door open. It was too late. Cleaver collapsed under the table. "You'll pay for this, Cleaver," I warned. "Forever."

The little man was in the middle of the diner looking around. Cleaver had sneaked back under the table. The man had a clipboard and was checking things on a list. He went behind the counter. He disappeared for a minute while he must have been poking around for mouse dirt or something on the floor.

Then he spoke across the counter to Granny Rubin. "Mrs. Stuart?"

"That's my daughter," she said. Not a word more.

"She around? I'm William Curtin, state health officer."

I answered, "She went over to Madison. She'll be back

by five." Maybe Mr. Curtin would go away and give us time to move Cleaver outside.

"It doesn't matter. I wanted to introduce myself. Mr. MacMurdo has retired."

Now I remembered that Mr. MacMurdo had told Mom six months ago it was his last visit. He was a real nice man. He'd poke around a little bit and have a cup of coffee with Mom or Linda. He put up a fresh sign that said the Good Luck Diner had an AA rating, et cetera. "You better watch out for the new man, whoever he is," Mr. MacMurdo told us. "He'll be gung ho for a while. I didn't see Cleaver today. I reckon he's under the counter minding his own business, or else your friends at the Golden Dragon have told you I'm in town and Cleaver is up the hill."

But the Yengs had left the Golden Dragon and moved to New Haven to take over a bigger place, leaving me without my best friend, Helen. We didn't know the new people at the Golden Dragon well enough to ask them to tell us when the state inspector showed up there.

Mr. Curtin walked around the diner, bending over and peeping behind things. "Looks nice out here," he told us. "I'll take a look at the kitchen now."

"The kitchen's okay," he told us as he came back. "Very nice, in fact." He stood beside booth number four writing on his clipboard. "You'd have an AA rating, except for the dog." Mr. Curtin pointed with his pen under the table. "Looks like a nice dog," he said.

"His name is Cleaver," Granny Rubin said. "He's a

33

genuine Bernese mountain dog. They're very special. He's the only one in town."

"I'm pleased to meet him. I'm sure he's a lovely dog, but he shouldn't be in the diner. He's a violation of the code."

"Mr. MacMurdo was very fond of Cleaver, too." Granny Rubin didn't say right out that he had purposely not noticed Cleaver under the counter, but she sort of implied it.

"I'm happy to be his friend, too. From the size of him, I definitely wouldn't want to be his enemy. But today I'm afraid I must report that he was situated in the dining area in violation of the regulation that no animals are allowed residence in places serving food. The state simply cannot permit it."

"Did you ever hear how Cleaver saved my daughter from the assailant?" Granny Rubin asked.

"I don't believe I have."

"Well, one evening," Granny Rubin began, "when Cleaver was still growing, this tough guy came in. Oh, you could tell the minute he came in the door. One of those bikers, with a beard and half crazy on drugs. My daughter Benedicta was cleaning up. He took a pistol from his pocket and made my daughter go behind the counter. He hadn't come just for the money, you could see. My daughter is a very brave woman. She yelled as loud as she could. It just happened that our dog, Cleaver, had come down the hill to walk back to the house with Benedicta. This isn't a safe section of the road, Mr. Curtin. It looks safe, but a bad quality of people comes by sometimes.

"That dog you saw under the table, only not so big, he jumped on that biker, ripped his black leather jacket to shreds and bit him hard on the shoulder right through the steel stuff he had on his jacket. The guy dropped his pistol and ran out the door, Cleaver snapping at him every step. The chief of police said he was a hero dog. That's what they called him in the papers, right there under his picture, a hero dog. Now my daughter leaves Cleaver here to look after Sarah and me when she has to go off for a while."

"I see," Mr. Curtin said. "I hadn't heard about that." He smiled. "There's a Bernese down the street from me in Belmont. The people who own him say he's as gentle as a kitten, wouldn't bite anyone."

"Only bad guys, Mr. Curtin."

Mr. Curtin drew a line through something he had written on his clipboard. He wrote something else on a clean piece of paper, signed the inspection card, and left it on the table with a folded piece of paper.

We watched him get in his car and drive off. "I left my glasses in the house, child," Granny Rubin said. "What's that he left?"

"It's the health card marked AA like always. On the paper it says, *'No dogs in diners!'*"

Cleaver came out from under the table to see if the bad guy had left. Granny Rubin held the paper under his nose. "See that, Cleaver? That means you."

—7—

"Really, Mama," Mom said after we had unloaded the supplies and Granny Rubin had told her about Mr. Curtin's visit. "That poor boy who came to rob me was more frightened than I was. All Cleaver did was hit the shelf with his head and knock some plates to the floor. He was the most scared one of all."

Granny Rubin smiled just a little bit. "You still have your permit, Benedicta. What were *you* going to tell the man, that Cleaver was in the diner to guard the hamburgers?"

"What will I tell him next December when Cleaver will still be under the table? I'm going to tack Mr. Curtin's note to the bulletin board. Two months a year Cleaver will be an up-the-hill dog."

"Mr. Curtin didn't believe Granny Rubin," I butted in. "I think he thought she was funny or something, or maybe he liked dogs."

"Don't be a know-it-all, Sarah," Granny said. "You

36

don't know what he believed. Get me another glass of iced tea and take care of the family that just drove up."

"Wait a minute, Sarah," Mom said. "I passed Mrs. Travis with Patricia on the way home. I pulled over to ask her about Billy. She wondered if you could bring Cleaver to visit with his tennis ball."

"Cleaver doesn't chase tennis balls anymore, Mom. But I'll walk him down to see Billy. Is he all right?"

"I don't think so. Mrs. Travis looked worried. Poor kid, this weather must make it worse."

Billy Travis was a little kid who lived down the road beyond the Michaelses'. He had some terrible disease which Mom said wasn't going to get any better. He spent all his life in bed or in a wheelchair. Last summer when Cleaver was younger and full of pep, Cori and I would take him down to visit with Billy, sometimes to sit with him for a little while if Mrs. Travis had to do an errand. Cori would throw the ball down the lawn and most of the time Cleaver would goof around and tease her with it. That made Billy smile. We let Billy throw it, which wasn't very far, and when Billy threw it, Cleaver brought it back and dropped it in his lap or beside the wheelchair where Billy's little sister picked it up for him. Then Cleaver sat and waited for Billy to throw it again.

Cori couldn't understand why Cleaver would bring the ball to Billy Travis but not to her. "It's because he's a boy," she complained. "Dogs do things for boys."

"That's not so. Cleaver isn't dumb. He figured out Billy couldn't chase him around the way you do."

The next morning I caught Cori before she skipped away to Margo's. "We have to take Cleaver down to see Billy Travis and maybe chase his ball. Come on, Cori. Call up Margo and tell her you'll be late this morning. You aren't doing anything all that important."

"Today is ice-cream day," Cori protested. "I have to help. We're making chocolate, vanilla, and fresh strawberry with our own berries. Anyway, Cleaver gave up on his ball. The only thing he'll chase now is a bone."

Cori had a mind of her own. She never agreed to anything right away. First, she had to protest. I didn't argue. I put Cleaver's leash on and told her to dig the ball out of the boot box we hadn't put into the attic yet.

"I told you he won't chase it, Sarah. You don't need me to throw it."

I still didn't say anything. Cleaver and I marched down the driveway and turned toward the Travises'. Cori raced past. "I'll wait for you at Billy's," she shouted.

The Travises were sort of rich. They had a big brick house halfway up the hill with a lot of trees in front and a lawn rolling all the way down to the road. Most people in Stanhope made a point of cutting their own lawns or, if they were too big, letting them grow to hay. But Mr. Travis had a yard service come from Hartford every week to look after the lawn and flowers and plants. Dad said it was two or three acres big.

Mrs. Travis rolled Billy out to the edge of the driveway and locked the chair. Billy looked really sick, a lot thinner than he had the last time we saw him. His head was pushed back and turned to one side. He had a tough time talking and we couldn't always understand him. Today he didn't say anything.

"You and Cori will have to toss the ball today, Sarah," Mrs. Travis said. "Billy isn't feeling so well these days. He's going to the hospital this afternoon. I thought a visit from Cleaver would please him." Mrs. Travis looked as though she had been crying a lot. Patricia was holding on to her mother's hand. Usually she made a lot of noise when Cleaver came to visit; this morning she was as quiet as a clam.

I unsnapped Cleaver's leash. He nuzzled Billy's lap to let him know he was there. Billy grabbed the heavy, soft fur under Cleaver's ears. He turned his head so he could watch. Cori heaved the tennis ball across the lawn. "Get it, Cleaver, go get it." Cleaver tore loose from Billy's grasp and thumped across the lawn. He forgot about his bum leg and extra pounds. He snapped up the tennis ball and brought it back to the wheelchair.

Patricia picked up the ball and smiled. She gave the ball to me. I tossed it as far as I could. Again Cleaver brought it back to Patricia.

We did this for half an hour or so, giving Cleaver a rest in the middle, until Billy closed his eyes and turned his head sideways.

"Thank you both," Mrs. Travis said. "This has done Billy a lot of good. He talks about Cleaver."

"We're making ice cream at the Michaelses' this morn-

39

ing, our own fresh strawberry. I'll bring some to Billy if that's all right," Cori offered.

"Would you like that, Billy?" Mrs. Travis asked her son. "When you're back home."

Billy made some little noises, and Mrs. Travis told Cori the ice cream would be very nice.

A couple of days later Mrs. Travis called Mom. Could she drive Cori and Cleaver and me over to the hospital? Billy wasn't doing too well. He talked about Cleaver, and the doctor thought a short visit would help. It was against the rules, Mrs. Travis said, but they would make an exception.

In the evening we piled into the back of the Toyota. At the hospital, they let us in the back entrance, Cleaver pulling like crazy on his leash and sniffing at all the new smells. Billy was in a separate room. He had a couple of tubes running from his arm and from under the sheet. He looked like a little wax child.

"Billy," Mrs. Travis whispered. "Billy, Cleaver has come for a visit. Cleaver is here." Billy opened his eyes halfway and saw Cleaver panting beside the bed. He reached out his hand. Cleaver put his front paws on the side of the bed and licked Billy's hand. Cleaver whined once and looked around at Cori to see what he was supposed to do next.

"Scratch his ears, Billy," Cori said. "Scratch his ears. He likes that."

Billy reached a little farther and ran his fingers over Cleaver's ear. He held on tight until Cleaver yipped and pulled away. A little smile came across Billy's face.

The next day Mom said Billy died during the night. There were some people at the counter I was looking after. I couldn't wait on them. I hurried out the back door and bawled. Granny Rubin left the register to come put her arm around me.

Mrs. Travis didn't ask, but Mom said she would take Cori and Cleaver and me to the service at the cemetery. We could stand at the back out of everybody's way.

There were an awful lot of people standing around the coffin listening to the preacher. Cleaver sat beside us, good as gold, except once when he whined. The preacher stopped for a minute. Mrs. Travis turned around. She smiled sadly and nodded. The preacher went on talking.

8

Cori came home early bringing an invitation from the Michaelses for a picnic on their lawn Sunday afternoon. If it rained, we should come the next Sunday. "I told them the diner was always closed on Sunday. Was that right, Mom?"

"You know that's right, Cori. Sundays are the days when your father is around," Mom said in a sarcastic tone.

"Aw, come on, Nettie, lay off for a while," Dad grumbled. "I was here this week, wasn't I?"

"Yes, you were, I have to admit," Mom said. "Not Monday or Tuesday or Wednesday or Thursday, but Friday evening when we didn't need you, you were here, big as life."

Dad turned around on the counter stool to face Mom. He looked at her seriously. "I made a mistake, Nettie," he said.

It sounded like the beginning of an argument. I held my breath. Cori looked up from her dessert at me. She was scared. "Excuse me," she said, slipping off her stool. "I have to go. I forgot something at the Michaelses'."

Dad reached out a big hand and pulled her to him. "I'm not going to fight and your mother here is not going to fight with me. Promise, Nettie?"

"Promise what? I keep my promises when I make them."

Dad winced. "Okay, no promise. What I was going to say was that I made two mistakes. One, I shouldn't have promised something I couldn't take care of, like helping out here in the evenings. Two, I shouldn't have put those new machines in at the college. They've been nothing but trouble."

"It's okay," Mom broke in. "Sarah and I can get along fine. I only wish you hadn't made a big to-do about coming back here to help. We sort of expected to have you here. I might have found a replacement for Linda. We'll make it until August, no matter what."

"The thing is," Dad went on, "I've had a good offer for the business, and I wanted to see what you all said about it. I'm working on something else, but I'm not going to tell you until I'm ready."

Mom frowned. She didn't like surprises. "What is it this time? Not a puppy farm, I hope. And not something to keep you away all the time. The girls need you—and so do I. And I'm not selling the diner. I've already told you that. I may lease it or something, but I'm not selling."

Dad stood up. "It's okay then. I'll sell the launderettes. Who wants to go to the pond?"

"I do," shouted Cori.

"You, too, Sarah?" Dad asked.

"I do, but I can't. I don't think my old bathing suit fits."

"Cut off those old jeans and wear a T-shirt," Mom said.

"Mom!" I shouted.

"Well, wear an undershirt, too."

"I'll straighten up here," Granny Rubin said. "Don't let the sharks get you," she warned Cori. She tickled her ribs until Cori screamed.

Cleaver wandered out from the kitchen. He looked dopey and tired. The heat was really getting to him.

"Come on, Cleaver. Want a ride? Let's go get in the car," Cori told him.

Cleaver knew what *car* meant, usually something good. Some days when Mom forgot to pull the hatchback down on the Toyota, Cleaver jumped inside and refused to get out. Now, tail wagging, he ran up the hill after Cori and planted himself in back of the Toyota.

Last year when it was even hotter, the town put some lights at the town beach and kept it open until ten o'clock. You weren't supposed to go out beyond where the lights reached, but kids did. One teenager had almost drowned a couple of weeks ago.

"Last one in is a rotten egg," Cori screamed as soon as the car stopped. She raced to the pond. Cleaver wasn't going to be the rotten egg. He charged into the water a couple of steps ahead of her. I got out and waited for Mom and Dad, but Dad started kissing Mom and she

44

kissed him back, so I went down to the beach by myself.

None of my friends from the seventh grade was there. Mostly it was boys in cutoff jeans like mine pushing and splashing and running around in circles showing off. It didn't do any good for the lifeguard to blow his whistle and tell them to keep it under control.

Cori and Cleaver swam out beyond the little kids' rope. Cleaver's white jaw and the touch of white on the top of his head were all you could see. When he was used to the water, Cori grabbed the fur on the back of his neck and Cleaver kept on paddling this way and that as though she weren't there. When Dad plunged in and swam underwater all the way out to under Cleaver, the big dog shook Cori loose and tried to climb on Dad's shoulders, scratching and whining to be held.

"What's he doing?" Mom asked. She had sat down on the sand beside me.

"It's hard to tell," I replied. "He's worried, I think. He'll pull Cori around, but with bigger people he wants to hold on himself. I don't know why. I guess he's jealous. Granny Rubin says he was the runt of the litter."

"I didn't know that," Mom said. "He's a pretty good dog, isn't he? Does he do more things than other dogs, do you suppose?"

"I don't suppose so. About the same as a golden retriever. But somehow Cleaver's different. It's like he's responsible for us. Maybe it's because he's part sheepdog or maybe it's because Dad wasn't around, or maybe it's because he has two places to live—in the diner and the house—and he's confused. He doesn't like to be very far away from us, that's for sure."

"Me, either," Mom said. "What do you suppose Dad is up to this time? I'll stop working in the diner if it's something I can help him with. The thing is, I never felt drawn to his laundry business. I'd rather work my fifteen hours in the Good Luck. What about you? In September would you just like to go to school? I mean, not work in the diner? Maybe it would bring your grades up. You'll need them if you go off to private school."

"I don't think so, Mom. I wasn't cut out for school. Other kids have jobs, too, and make straight A's. Anyway, I want to go to the high school."

"This hasn't been a good year for you, has it?"

I felt uncomfortable when Mom kept poking away at me. I sometimes let the diner be my excuse because I wasn't interested in doing my work. Now maybe things were going to change and I wouldn't have the Good Luck any longer as an excuse. I shrugged and didn't answer.

Now Mom said, "You're captain of the hockey team next year, aren't you? How come you didn't tell me?"

"I don't know."

"Do you have any more secrets you haven't shared?"

I shook my head. "I guess I'll go in now."

"Your father will be around more this month, I'm pretty sure. You'll have some free time. Is there something you'd really like to do?"

I recalled what Mrs. Porter had said: "Keep up with your writing, Sarah. I have faith in you."

"Two things, I guess. I'd like to do some stories for Mrs. Porter—and the other thing, well, I'd like to—I can't tell you." It was a wish I had made when I saw a shooting star.

9

At two o'clock Sunday afternoon we set out for the Michaelses' picnic. I walked behind with Mom. Dad and Granny Rubin were laughing about something we couldn't hear. Cori had left right after breakfast. "To get ready for the picnic," she had said, and had run across the field, Cleaver on the leash thundering ahead. Cori had whispered something in his ear when she snapped on the leash. Cleaver began to dance around. He crashed through the door as soon as Cori began to open it.

"Do you realize, Sarah," Mom was saying, "this picnic is the first time I've gone visiting since long before your father left, even to a movie at the mall? What kind of life have I been leading, anyway? I'm a slave to the Good Luck Diner. No wonder Granny says I'm crazy. Maybe the road people *should* take it away."

The work was getting to my mother. All she wanted to do on Sundays was sleep. It didn't do any good for

Granny and me to tell her to take it easy. I tried to cheer her up. "It's a pretty dress, Mom," I told her. It was red and white with tie straps at the shoulders. She was wearing white sandals I hadn't seen before.

"Is it? I bought it on sale a couple of years ago and never wore it."

"It looks good on you," I went on. Most of the time in the kitchen Mom wore pants and a T-shirt and a ribbon holding her hair back. Whenever I thought of her, that was how I saw her. It was hard to get beyond that picture of her, I realized: Mom in her T-shirts bending over the worktable or the stove or pushing plates of food through the window to Linda and me.

I put my arm around her. Cori and I were lucky to have her for a mother. Some of the kids had fancy moms who drove big station wagons to pick them up at school, a couple of little blond kids in the back along with, maybe, a stupid Irish setter slobbering all over the windows. Then on to the dentist to get the braces checked or ballet lessons or, in the winter, to Mrs. Hilborn's private indoor pool for swimming lessons (sign up three years ahead of time). It was the way the kid treated the mother and the way the mom acted toward the kid that got me, a lot of "darlings" and fake smiles.

Mom never came to get us, and we never expected her to. When we came into the Good Luck, she said, "Hi." If she was cross she only nodded. But we knew what we had with Mom. She was real. No foolishness. She loved us and when she told us how much we mattered to her and how lucky she was to have two girls like Cori and me, we believed her. I tightened my arm around her waist.

Mom patted my hand. "Well, aren't we a pair? You're almost as big as I am, and I'm not talking about your weight. You'll be a big woman when you grow up. You have Dad to thank for that."

There were a couple of cars at the vegetable stand, although it was still too early in the season for the Michaelses to have much produce to sell—only lettuce, radishes, early peas, along with the eggs and flowers and baked goods. The real stuff from the garden, Cori informed me, was ten days to two weeks from being ready. She and Margo had something special they wanted us to see. That was why the Michaelses were having a picnic—so the girls could show off. Cori wouldn't say what it was. "You'll see. It's a surprise," she said. "I can't tell you, or Cleaver, either. It's partly his picnic, too."

Mrs. Michaels was bringing out a couple of pies to the stand. She had a limp from a childhood accident that hadn't healed right. She was older than Mom, her hair streaked with gray and wrinkles around the eyes. They had a couple of grown children, Cori kept telling us, a daughter who was a nurse in Alaska and a boy in the navy who would be home for the picnic. Margo was their love child, Cori confided.

"Like you, Cori," I had said in a nasty voice.

"Jerk," Cori snapped back.

Next to the stand was a blue-and-white-striped awning

stretched out on four poles. Under the awning were two card tables and some folding wooden chairs. A slate was propped up in front of the awning announcing home-made ice cream.

VANILLA, CHOCOLATE,

AND *FRESH* STRAWBERRY.

LEMONADE AND COOKIES.

"How are you, Nettie, and Ed, and Mrs. Rubin?" Mrs. Michaels greeted them. "This is what the girls wanted you to see. It's their first day in business. They made the ice cream and the cookies. *And* three pans of brownies this morning. It looks like they have gone into business with a vengeance. Allen was coming home with his girlfriend, Beth, from the submarine station, so Fred thought we ought to have a celebration picnic. We'll sit over there." Mrs. Michaels pointed to a couple of blankets spread under a big sugar maple. "I hope you won't mind if we jump up to tend the stand."

Mr. Michaels came out of the house with a tub of ice and some plastic containers of lemonade. "Is this where you want it?" he asked Margo, putting the tub under the awning.

"What do you think, Cori?" Margo asked. The two of them gave it a lot of thought before they agreed the tub was all right where Mr. Michaels had put it down.

"And the ice cream, Dad," Margo asked. "Please, out-side?"

"I told you it will be mush if you try to keep it cold

51

in the ice. You'll have to take the orders and go into the freezer." Mr. Michaels turned toward us. "Hi," he said. "It looks like I'm doing all the work for this café. Well, let's see how they do. Beer, Ed? How about you, Nettie? And you, Mrs. Rubin?"

"Could I have some of the lemonade?" Granny asked Cori.

"I'll have one, too," I said.

"That will be a dollar each," Cori told us.

"What a cheapskate," I said.

"Never mind, Sarah. I'll pay for it. Here you are, Cori." Granny Rubin handed her two dollars, which Cori put in a toy cash register that was half mine.

The grown-ups started talking. I went over to sit next to Cleaver, whose leash was tied short to the maple tree where he couldn't get at all the food Mrs. Michaels had spread out on the blankets. He nuzzled me to scratch his head while he kept his eyes fixed on the food. We were a couple of fat outcasts.

Another car drove up. A woman got out to study the pies and lettuce and eggs. "Are the eggs fresh?" she asked.

"Laid last night," Mrs. Michaels answered sharply.

"I'll take a dozen." The woman turned to the café. "Oh, look, Jack. Homemade ice cream. Fresh strawberry."

"Yes, ma'am," Margo piped up. "Our own berries. Cone or dish? Either one a dollar."

"Well, what do you say, Jack?"

Jack muttered something I couldn't hear.

"Jack says he wants a cone. Two strawberry cones."

Cori scooted to the house for the cones. She put two more dollars in our cash register.

That was how it went on all afternoon. I ate my sandwich and pie, sneaking Cleaver a smidgin when Mom wasn't looking. The grown-ups didn't pay me any attention. When I asked Cori if they needed help she told me not very politely she and Margo could take care of their business. Allen and Beth sat down for a while, but they were interested only in each other and went inside.

I felt out of it—lumpy and rejected and stupid and out of it. More than that, I realized, I was jealous. Cori had something exciting to do and a friend to do it with. In addition, she was as thin as a straw. Now, she was getting rich, too. By four o'clock she and Margo had sold out completely. They were dividing up the money into thirds, one third for each of them and a third for the Michaelses for the supplies. It was more than I made working in the diner.

I remembered again what Mrs. Porter had said. "The last stories weren't so good. I can't tell you why, exactly. You're the writer and it will come to you if you keep at it. Write about yourself, Sarah. There's no one else you know so well to write about. You will always have something in your head to use." I had already arranged the picnic in my head. I'd start tomorrow and keep at it. I'd have something for myself.

"Now, for the big surprise," Margo said. "Something

for Cleaver the Magic Dog. Are you ready, Cori?" she shouted.

"Ready," came a voice from the back of the house.

"Are you ready, Cleaver?" Margo asked Cleaver. "Ready for homemade banana ice cream?" She slipped the leash. Cori came from the corner of the house with a bowl of ice cream, a brownie on top.

Cleaver sniffed around. He licked a few sandwich crumbs from the blankets. Then he smelled the banana ice cream. He plunged toward Cori. He didn't stop when he came to her. He went right over her. Cori went on her back, the ice cream on top of her new pink dress. Cleaver started to lick the ice cream. Cori howled and tired to shove him off and get to her feet. Cleaver pushed her down and went on licking. He saved the brownie for last.

I suddenly felt a lot better. I really had something to write about.

—10—

The Winnebago was still a sore point with Mom. It was the first thing Dad did when he walked out, bought a big Winnebago to live in. "That ridiculous mastodon," Mom called it. Dad still used it for his laundry business. It was cluttered up now with tools and pieces of washers and dryers. There wasn't room for it in the garage, so there it sat on the hill under the sycamore tree.

Mom asked Dad to take the Toyota, which she almost never used, and to get rid of the elephant. "Or at least use it for a doghouse and get Cleaver from under my feet."

Cleaver thought the Winnebago was the best thing ever invented next to food. When Dad was putting tools or stuff in or taking them out, Cleaver made the Winnebago his place—not in back, where he had a couple of bunks he could crawl into, but up on the front seat stretched from side to side or sometimes sitting behind the wheel like the king of the mountain.

"The day you sell the Good Luck we'll leave the kids with your mother and take off for a year or two in the Winnebago," Dad teased. "I'll clean it up for us. We'll sleep all day and let Cleaver drive. What do you say, Nettie?"

Mom didn't like foolish talk. "How do you think it makes me feel," she asked, "seeing your escape wagon parked right outside the door?"

Dad never got mad. His feelings were hurt sometimes, but he never raised his voice. "Why do you say a thing like that, Nettie? Come out for a weekend and you'll see how great it is."

"That'll be the day," Mom snapped.

When Mom and Dad were separated he had Cori and me on weekends and took us places in the Winnebago; if the weather was bad we stayed in the parking place next to the launderette in Stanhope. Cori and Cleaver liked it better than I did. I was embarrassed to be seen living in a parking lot. And the bunks were too small. Cori fit better in the narrow bunk, and Cleaver had the front seat all to himself at night. When we traveled, he had to sit in back—but he had to have the window cracked so he could sniff where he was going.

The week after the picnic Dad was in the diner every evening except Tuesday. That made Mom as nervous as not having him there at all. By now she was used to having things her way. Not that Dad tried any longer to boss her around in her kitchen, but he did have sug-gestions for doing things that he had learned from running the diner himself for ten years. Like on Thursday when he came in with a mess of Lake Sebago salmon, all cleaned and filleted.

"What am I supposed to do with those?" Mom demanded. "It's macaroni-special night. Sarah has already made the sign." Every night Mom had a special and, when she was home, Cori made a sign with Magic Markers to stick to the door. This summer I was making the signs.

"Can't she make another sign?" Dad argued. "These are fresh frozen from Frank's freezer. He couldn't get rid of them."

"That's not much of a recommendation. Who's Frank?"

"A guy I met. Look, Nettie, all I'm asking is for the use of the broiler when someone orders salmon. That's not so much to ask, is it?"

"I guess not," Mom yielded. "Be sure you turn the ventilating fan up high. I never did like the smell of fried fish in my kitchen."

"Broiled, Nettie, broiled."

So I made a sign, and salmon must have sounded good to a lot of people. It sold out by eight o'clock.

"We didn't even get any for ourselves," Mom said. "How about that?" She had taken over the counter to let him have the kitchen all to himself. You could see she was pretty pleased.

Granny Rubin and Cleaver were both pleased, too. Granny because she sensed that Mom and Dad were getting to be good friends again and Cleaver because he did get a piece of salmon—the last fillet, which had dried out, so Dad gave it to him.

"What do you say we go up to Twisted Lake Sunday?" Dad asked. "The boys are having a fishing party and the wives and kids are invited."

The "boys" were something new to us. Granny got her question in first, the way she generally did. "What boys, Ed?"

"Oh, a couple of men with RVs I met along the way."

"What way, Ed?" Mom wanted to know.

"Oh," Dad said, uncomfortable. "A couple of times last year I went fishing when I was lonely and met them and we talked. I see them around."

"These are men who drive their RVs to work, too?" Mom asked.

Dad didn't like the inquisition. "Look," he said. "I got lonely once in a while and went up to Sebago or down to the Cape to go fishing. Sometimes I took Sarah and Cori. A couple of times I just went. That's all. Except that I ran into Frank—Frank Lawton—today who said he and a couple of others are going fishing on Sunday with their families and did I want to come along."

"Count me out," Mom said. "You know how I feel about that monster."

Dad leaned across the table to take Mom's hand. "I'll make a deal, Nettie. You and the girls come up to the lake—no room for you, Granny Rubin—and I'll sell the Winnebago and buy a sports car. How about that?"

"He's got you there, Benedicta," Granny Rubin hooted.

What Dad said brought Mom up short. She gave it some thought before she answered. "We could take the Toyota," she began.

"The Winnebago, leaving Saturday night at nine o'clock."

"Cori is sleeping over at Margo's Saturday night," Mom said, stalling.

"She can sleep over some other night. I want to show Frank and the boys my family."

"Okay," Mom said. "Shake! When are you selling the Winnebago?"

"I've already sold it," Dad laughed. "To Frank. He's picking it up on Monday."

Saturday night Cleaver took it in his head that Frank and the boys wanted to meet him, too. No one was smarter than Cleaver in knowing how to stay in a car when everyone wanted him out. Granny Rubin, who usually sided with Cleaver when he had a problem, tried to scold him out. "Selfish dog," she said. "Let them have some privacy. They don't need the family dog. You stay home with me. I'll make you a pie crust." Cleaver paid no attention. He was in the driver's seat. Cori reached over and smacked Cleaver on the butt. "Get out!" she screamed. Cleaver growled. He wasn't used to being abused.

It was Mom who gave in first. "Oh, let him come. He always went with you three before."

"Because you made me take him," Dad reminded her.

We made a settlement with Cleaver. He agreed to move out of the front seat to the back of the Winnebago for a chunk of pepperoni. He took his place beside the window and yipped to have it cracked open.

The air was cool by the time we reached the state park at the top of Twisted Lake. You could smell the pine trees. Cori and I were as excited as Cleaver. I couldn't remember when all of us had gone off on an expedition. It seemed there was always something to keep us busy at the diner. As soon as Dad moved the Winnebago between three other Winnebagos and gave the horn a blast, Cori slid open the door and Cleaver dashed out, paused to get his bearings, and headed for the lake.

Down by the shore some figures were sitting on logs around a fire. A man stood up and strode over to greet us. It turned out to be Frank Lawton. He took us all earnestly by the hand, laughed when Cleaver shook water all over him, and drew us to the camp fire. There were three other families, the men and women in checked flannel woodsmen shirts and eight kids in old clothes and dirty sneakers. No girls my age, just a boy about thirteen who looked sort of friendly. The kids settled down with their coat hangers to roast marshmallows which they had saved for our arrival. The grown-ups were busy getting acquainted. I noticed that Mom seemed right at home.

It was long after midnight when we headed for our bunks. Cori had fallen asleep with her head on Dad's lap. Frank said he and Morris had caught some breakfast trout before dark which they had strung in the lake. Evelyn had made a bag of doughnuts. We were put in charge of coffee.

Cori had the top bunk over me and Mom wedged herself into her bunk over Dad. Cleaver took the front seat. "You both sleep in the morning," I told Mom and Dad. "I'll let Cleaver out and put on a couple of pots of coffee."

"Okay," Dad said. "You're in charge."

Early in the morning I heard soft talk in the trees. It sounded like a couple of the kids were going swimming. The water was really cold. I had put my foot in before we went to bed. But I liked the idea anyway. I let Cleaver out and looked around. Mom's bunk was empty. Down below she had crawled into Dad's bunk. She was jammed up against his back holding on for dear life.

Every year in July the carnival showed up in Stanhope. Some of it was there to start with, like the jelly and cake contests, the homemade quilts, and the different local raffles, but the real carnival, the part with rides and flickering lights and noisy loudspeakers and the arcade of games of chance and the fried-food stands and the tough-looking guys with tattoos and leather vests, was Sam Dominici's All-American Road Show, which traveled, the posters said, all over New Jersey, New York, and New England.

Last summer when Dad was on his sabbatical, as Mom called it, Cori and I decided that we wouldn't go without Mom *and* Dad because it was one of the few things we ever did as a family. Granny Rubin and Linda, or whoever else was waitressing, took over the Good Luck for a Saturday and we all went to the carnival early and stayed late. Dad did ask Mom last year if she'd come along like always. She gave him a nasty look and shook her head. "I'm not a weekend wife, Ed," she told him. Cori and I said we'd rather see a movie.

This year it was different. Mom wouldn't go, but she could have if she wanted to. Granny Rubin told her to close the kitchen and go, she'd tend the counter, but Mom wouldn't have that. "You go on with the girls, Ed. An August vacation will be enough for me." When I really thought about it, I realized the Stanhope July Carnival wasn't the greatest thing in my life any longer, either, but I didn't vote against going. Maybe it had changed from two years ago.

Cori and Cleaver were all for going. It wasn't clear whether Cleaver decided for himself or Cori whispered in his ear. After his breakfast Cleaver collapsed under the worktable to digest his food while he waited for the rest of us to have the all-star power breakfast Dad pre-pared—sugared French toast with syrup and chocolate milk, enough sugar to burn up the whole town, Mom commented. In the meantime, Cleaver fell asleep. Even when the three of us said good-bye to Mom and Granny Rubin, Cleaver didn't lift an eyebrow. It was after we were out the door and a hundred yards up the hill that Cleaver discovered that he had been left behind. He hit the door, Mom said, like a battering ram. When it didn't break, he set in to howl and bark. We heard the thump, then the noise.

"What's going on?" Dad asked.

"It's just Cleaver," I said. "He wants to go, too."

Usually the farther away you get from a sound, the

less you hear it, but not today. Cleaver's yelps were just as loud at the top of the hill as at the bottom.

We climbed into the Toyota, Cleaver still howling. Granny Rubin stuck her head out the door. "Benedicta says she can't take it, he's not going to stop," she called. "She's afraid if she lets him out, he'll take off for the parade grounds."

"We better take him, Dad," Cori said. "I'll look after him, except when I go on the rides; then you can hold him. There's a dog show," she added innocently. "We can enter him in the contests and events."

"What do you mean, a dog show? Who told you that?" Dad demanded.

"It was in the paper. The county animal-rescue league, something like that, is having a dog show in the afternoon. 'Bring your dog,' it said. I bet you Cleaver will clean up all the prizes."

"I don't suppose you told Cleaver about the carnival," I said sarcastically.

"Only about the dog show."

"Tell Mom to let him out. Get his short leash, Cori," Dad ordered.

Cleaver roared up the hill like a black tornado. He never missed a step as he jumped into the Toyota. He didn't say thank you; he just sat there waiting for us to hurry up and take him to the dog show.

Nothing much had changed with the All-American Road Show except maybe some of the tattoos. The rides, we discovered, were the same. The Crazy House was two years dirtier and the rides got shorter the longer the lines. The loudspeakers were louder. Right off, Cori lost three dollars of her ice-cream money on a stupid Duck-a-Duck game and Dad found out he wasn't as good a pitcher as he thought he was in knocking down wooden milk bottles.

By noon we had enough of everything. It was time to go home and start getting ready for next year by forgetting about what a disappointment this year's carnival was. "We can't," Cori protested. "The dog show. Cleaver has to get his blue ribbons."

"Okay," Dad sighed. "I'll buy your lunch. What's it to be, hot dogs and a drink? Go find us a place under that tree."

Cleaver trotted after us to the shade, Cori carrying a drinking cup full of water. He had been awfully good all morning, marching in step right behind us without a whimper or a single tug of his leash, sitting patiently beside Dad when Cori and I went on the Surf Boat or the Rockaround and the Double Ferris Wheel.

Dad handed out the lunch. "Nothing for you, Cleaver," he said. He took a closer look at Cleaver's mouth. He frowned. "What's that on his snout?" He smelled. "Cotton candy!" he exclaimed. 'I didn't see him get any. Did you, Cori? Sugar is bad for dogs."

Cori shook her head. "Me, either."

A mother with a couple of kids sat down next to us with their hot dogs and cola and cotton candy. The kid next to Cleaver was screaming at his mother that he wanted root beer, not cola. He was holding his cotton candy toward Cleaver, who lifted his head and bit off a chunk without the kid's noticing. Only a chunk. Cleaver didn't push his luck.

Dad looked with amazement at what had happened. "All morning," he said, "that dog has been helping himself to cotton candy. And no one noticed. I could train him to be a professional pickpocket. Should we tell the mother?"

"No," said Cori. "She'd start yelling about germs. Don't worry, Cleaver only has good germs."

The dog show was for mutts that the animal-rescue league had found homes for. It wasn't the place for an all-American Swiss Bernese mountain dog. Some of the dogs were even cuter than Cleaver, who had grown up to be more handsome than cute. And the kids were all younger than Cori.

"This isn't for you, Cori," Dad said. "We'll take Cleaver to the Bernese dog show up in Massachusetts next spring. He's not a show dog, but he can talk to his relatives."

"No way," Cori resisted. "The paper said bring your dog. We don't care if you're a thoroughbred, do we, Cleaver?"

Embarrassed, Dad and I stood far away as Cori entered Cleaver in the tricks competition. A sort of terrier won that, paws down. Next came the obedience contest. When Cori tried to enter Cleaver, a woman in a green jacket wanted to know what kind of dog he was. "All kinds," Cori replied, which wasn't altogether a lie, because Bernese had a little bit of everything in them once upon a time.

Cleaver didn't know how to obey, except to sit. The woman in the green jacket expected more than sitting down. A poodle mixture won that contest.

The last contest for Cleaver to fail was best groomed. Cori had brought her brush and she gave Cleaver a good working over, but he looked sort of silly with cotton candy lipstick around his mouth. A Labrador-collie was judged the best groomed, and that was the end of the dog show. The little kids ran off with their dogs, leaving Cori and Cleaver behind.

The woman in the green jacket pulled a blue ribbon from her pocket. "I wonder what this was for," she said. "I must have forgotten an event." She shrugged and turned to Cori. "Would you like this, young lady? It can be for whatever your dog is best at."

Cori snatched the blue ribbon and tied it to Cleaver's collar. "There you are, Cleaver. Best family dog, that's you."

—12—

Gilberto had come to the elementary school in the third or fourth grade. He didn't speak much English, but by the time he reached the seventh grade you could hardly tell he came from Central America. Except for his name, and he couldn't do anything about that. The kids at school could never get it straight; a lot of them didn't want to. You were supposed to say Heelberto, or Heel; not Jilberto or Geelberto or Gillberto. The boys thought it was funny to have three pronunciations for your name. They thought it was the funniest thing you ever heard to say, "Hey, Heel, I mean Jeel, or did I mean Geel? I don't know what I mean. Which one are you?" Then they would start in on Gool and Gull and Jelly and any other idiot sound they could think of. For a long while, Gil tried to educate them. That was a waste of time and eventually he gave up.

The girls were better. Some of them still giggled when a teacher called on Heel to answer in class and Stan, a real dummy in the back row, whispered, "Heel's a heel," which cracked him and his dopey friend Anthony up for the rest of the day.

Once he straightened out his English, Gilberto was the brightest boy in class. When my grades started to slip again toward the end of the year, I'd leave for school early some mornings and wait for Gilberto to show up to give me some help with algebra. He made more sense than Mr. Tracy, who had been teaching for almost fifty years and was a little confused. Thanks to Gil I ended up with a C instead of a D or flunking the course.

The Mendoza family lived in the bottom apartment of a two decker in what I guess you'd call the poor section of Stanhope, the part of town where most of the mill workers lived back when Stanhope was a mill town. The town didn't really have a rich section or a poor section any longer. The really rich families lived in big houses out in the country, and the not-so-well-off lived in two deckers and three deckers in the section called Bronton, after the Bronton Mills.

The Mendozas were refugees from El Salvador. The church committee in Stanhope had found an apartment and jobs for them when they fled their country to keep from being shot by either the army or the rebels, Gilberto wasn't sure. There were three kids in the school and one at home. Gil was the oldest.

After school let out for the summer, Gilberto always had some sort of job, so I didn't see him at the playing fields in Little League or summer soccer. I was surprised when he pushed his bike up to the side of the diner and parked it. He had two plastic milk crates strapped to the back.

He seemed pretty glad to see someone from school. "Hi, Sarah," he said. "This is your diner, eh, the one you said you worked in, I mean?"

I nodded. "It's hot out there, isn't it?"

"You bet. Do you have any lemonade?"

"Only lemon drink. It's in a bottle. It's not very good. We have soft drinks."

"Yeah, but they leave you thirsty after ten minutes."

"Wait a second. I'll see if Mom has any lemons. I'll make you a lemonade."

Mom peered through the opening at Gil. "What a nice-looking boy. Come help yourself. You'll need two lemons to get it to taste like anything."

I handed the lemonade to Gil and watched him take a sip.

"It's good, real good," Gil said. "How much?"

"How much, Mom?" I shouted.

"It's okay."

Gil reached in to his jeans pocket. "I'd rather pay, please."

"It's all right, Mom says. She'll collect the next time. What are the milk crates for?"

Gil stuffed a dollar bill back into his pocket. "I have my own delivery service, did you know? I deliver after school and all day during summer. All over town."

"I never saw you at the market."

"Not at the supermarket, at Anderson's. They sell by

phone and deliver to old people and shut-ins. They used to have their own delivery van, but that cost too much. Now they have me."

I was curious. "Do you make much?" I asked.

"It depends. It's a dollar a delivery, fifty cents for Mr. Anderson and fifty for me. Some days the tips are good, other days you don't get any. I can't figure it out. Anything helps at home. My mother does sewing and my father is night janitor at the high school. Sometimes we all get homesick. We had a little restaurant at home, sort of like the diner."

"You can't go home?"

"Sure, we can go home," he said bitterly. "We might not live long there, but we can go home. Both sides have it in for our town. Don't ask me why, we don't understand it; the army and the rebels both want to wipe it out. My father says it's not personal. Just political. Some day we'll go home, I guess. We may have to if we don't get a permit. Your country says we aren't here legally."

Gil finished his lemonade. He reached in for the ice cubes. "To keep me cool," he laughed. "I'll drop by again if I'm out this way. I don't come out this way often. Take care, Sarah."

Mom came out, wiping her hands on her apron. She had been making hamburgers. "What was that all about?"

"It was Gil. It's spelled *G I L*."

"I know," Mom said. "I went to school, too. He's in your class?"

"Yeah. The kids still tease him about his name. He's

from Central America. He's a refugee. Like my grand-parents?"

"Like Mama and Papa, yes. He's from El Salvador?"

I nodded. "He says they shoot people in his town for no reason. Does that sound right, Mom?"

"Yes," Mom said. "For no reason, just because you're in the way, I suppose. Or they want to try out their guns."

"They may have to go back. They don't have a permit to be here. They have to be real refugees who the army or somebody really wants to kill at home, something like that. It sounds crazy."

"I think the Mendozas have to *prove* they will be in danger if they return. I don't see how that works, unless you actually go home and get shot. You're right, it's a crazy world."

Gil Mendoza came in about a week later. Cleaver heard us talking and came out to greet Gil. He liked to keep track of family friends. Gil ran his hands over his coat. "He's a nice dog, you can see," Gil said. "We had a dog at home, I remember, a little brown dog that showed up. We had to leave it behind. I hope someone looked after it."

"How are things going?" I asked.

"With the permit?"

"Yeah, how's it going?"

"There's a hearing next week. My mother says we should move somewhere else and hide. My father says that wouldn't be right. We must go by the rules, if we want to stay here. See you later."

72

We didn't see Gil later. "What happened to that nice boy from El Salvador?" Mom asked one day.

"I don't know, Mom. Maybe he had to go back home."

"Hmm," Mom said. "I was thinking he could help out here with you and Cori come school time. We could have a Latin American special. You be sure to ask him if you see him."

For some reason what Mom said made me feel pretty good. Gil was a neat person to have for a friend.

—13—

Mom and I had hardly finished with the breakfast rush when one of those little tourist buses, the ones that sit high and look like a plastic toy, pulled up to the Good Luck. "Hey, Mom," I yelled. "Drink your coffee quick. Here comes a bus load."

"Good grief," I heard Mom sigh. "It's always something. I was going to get my hair cut this morning. It's falling all over my face."

I was watching the little bus. "Hold on, there's only one person getting out. Maybe it's to use the bathroom."

"Did you put in a roll of paper towels and toilet paper?"

"Yes, Mom. And I'll check at noon and before supper." The bathroom was another of my jobs I hoped Dad would take over when he had his schedule straight.

A Japanese girl—I couldn't be sure how old she was—came in. She looked around uncertainly.

"Would you like the bathroom?" I asked. "It's over there."

The girl shook her head. She was dressed as though she were going to play tennis—pleated skirt, thick white socks, and a sweatshirt saying YALE. She had a little microphone around her neck like the ones the television announcers use. She kept staring around without a word. At last she asked, "This is a real diner?"

"Yes, it is."

"Not one you made to look like a diner, but a real one?"

What was going on? "Where you are is real. Once it was a streetcar in New Haven. The kitchen in back was added on."

"I see. It is not a train car, but a trolley car. That is almost the same. Are you the owner?"

I shook my head. I wondered if she was thinking of buying the Good Luck to take back to Japan. Mom would be rich instantly. "My mother is," I replied.

"Could I speak with her, please?"

She *was* going to buy the diner. "Mom," I called. "Someone wants to talk to you."

Mom came out, pushing her hair back. Cleaver tagged along, curious. He sniffed once at the girl, who backed off scared, and he returned to the kitchen.

"You are the owner, yes?" The girl's English had been perfect. Now I noticed that it was a little different.

"I have what may seem a strange request. I must apologize for my English." She *was* going to offer to buy the

75

diner, I was certain of it now. The Japanese tourists had decided to buy it. What was Mom going to say? And Granny Rubin? She would never go along, I'd bet on that.

"My name is Mitsue Yamata. I am a student at Yale University in my second year. I am a student of American studies. I will go home to teach about your country to people in my country." Breathless, she paused to see if Mom understood her. "My father has a tour business in Tokyo. This year he has put me in charge of a tour bus in New England. I have decided not to go to the usual places. My tours will go to everyday American places, not tourist places. Do you understand?"

Mom nodded.

"I saw a picture of your diner in the newspaper. Your diner is an ordinary place, is it not?"

Mom laughed a little. "Yes, a very ordinary place."

"Good. I will show my group an American diner where regular people eat."

So it was breakfast they wanted. All that talk was about breakfast. How many were in the bus? We could only seat twenty-four people at a time.

"Do you reserve the whole diner?" Mitsue Yamata asked next.

"I never have," Mom said. "It's not fair to my regular customers."

"I see. There are twenty-one of us. Are you very occupied in the evening?"

"Not after eight o'clock."

Mitsue smiled. "Ah-ha. We will return at eight for our

American supper. Now, my special request. Can you serve us a typical diner supper? You choose for us, please, so I can assure my group this is an authentic meal. We will not need a menu, please. Can you do that?"

Mom looked puzzled. Lots of men came in and just said, "The usual," but we knew what the usual was because they had been having it five mornings a week for years. "I guess I can. Everything here is authentic. Are there some things you don't eat?"

"We eat everything. It would be impolite if we did not. Until eight o'clock, then. We are going to a cow dairy farm, a covered bridge, and a school for the blind. Good day."

"Wasn't that something?" Mom said. She sat at the counter while I poured her a cup of coffee. I took the last doughnut from the case for myself. Mom gave me a hard look, so I put it back. "You've lost some weight in this heat, Sarah. Keep it up. Get me a piece of paper. It would have been easier if they had taken the menu," she complained. "What do you suppose they think is authentic diner food? I don't know what that is."

"Baked beans, I guess. Hamburger with pickle relish or hot dogs. Does that go with beans?"

"Well enough. Fried chicken and corn bread. I can handle that," Mom said. "My macaroni special I can make ahead of time."

I was excited. "I tell you what I'll do. I'll run down to the Michaelses'. Margo and Cori can make a couple of cans of strawberry ice cream for dessert."

"That's a good idea. Dad said he was coming home

early today. We'll leave something for him to make. Tell Cori to come home by six. We'll get her to make plate menus and help out."

"Chowder, that's what I'll make," Dad said. "A New England clam and fish chowder." He studied Mom's menu. "It looks like a great meal, Nettie. I hope there will be some left over for me."

At eight o'clock Mitsue Yamata drove her little bus up to the side of the diner. Inside, the last customers, except for a couple of kids at the corner of the counter, were leaving. Cori had strung out her colored birthday streamers and made twenty-one menus on colored construction paper.

Mitsue led her tourists in. They came up to Mom and Dad and Cori and me and made little bows. The men wore white shorts and white shirts and white tennis hats with green brims. They all had black camera bags slung over their shoulders. The women were dressed the same, but with white skirts and no camera bags. The kids were dressed like tidy American kids. We smiled and Mitsue, who had a seating list, led them to the booths. Sixteen sat in booths, while Mitsue and the others ate at the counter.

It was hard to tell if they really liked what we had prepared, but Mitsue assured us the meal was a huge success. "We had no lunch," she told Mom, "only a soft drink and peanut-butter crackers. Listen to them, they are saying this is a really fine meal—and so cheap! If you could give me the recipe for the macaroni and the chowder, it would please them very much."

When Mom had written the recipes down, our marketing expert, Cori Stuart, put a cover on the two sheets of paper: THE GOOD LUCK DINER RECIPE BOOK.

The ice cream was finished and out came the cameras. Pictures of themselves, pictures of their friends, pictures of us, together and singly, pictures of us with the tour leader, Mitsue Yamata. About then Granny and Cleaver came down the hill to welcome the Japanese visitors. Pictures of Granny Rubin and Cleaver.

A little Japanese boy, seven or eight, latched on to Cleaver. He scooted past his mother and ran up to our dog. "It's okay," I said. "He's gentle." Mitsue translated what I said, and the kid put out his hand. Cleaver gave it a good lick. He could taste the ice cream and the hamburger juice. He looked expectantly at the kid for the other hand. "Wait a second," I said. Mom had put aside some hamburger for my supper. I slapped it on a plate and brought it out to the boy. "A little bit at a time," I told Mitsue, who passed the message on to the kid.

Cleaver sat down politely. He took the bits of hamburger as gently as he could. He licked his whiskers to show how grateful he was. Every camera in the diner was trained on Cleaver and the Japanese boy. With each bite, Cleaver edged closer. When the hamburger was gone, he licked the plate and the kid's hand again. The boy looked at his parents for approval. Cleaver stood up. He lifted his head high and slurped the boy in the face.

At that the boy's dad really went to work, taking about twenty rolls of film. Then Mitsue clapped her hands for her group to get in line so they could bow and shake hands with each of us. The boy and his dad were last. The kid couldn't keep his eyes off Cleaver. Mitsue paid the bill and told the group to get a move on.

The boy's dad took the camera from his shoulder. He said something to Mitsue. It sounded like an order. She nodded. He handed the camera over to me along with a business card. I took it. "Do I take a picture of him and his boy?" I asked Mitsue.

"No, the camera is for you. That is Mr. Kiora. He hopes you will enjoy it, and he would be grateful to you to take some pictures of Cleaver every year to send to his boy. It is a very good camera. You must take it without protesting. To refuse would be impolite. Anyway, he has another one in his bag."

—14—

"Are you sure you have enough clothes for Maine?" Mom fretted. "We only have this week to outfit you two."

"Granny Stuart doesn't expect anything fancy. All we need is shorts and a sweatshirt and a couple of pairs of sneakers, thing like that."

"You never went off for a month before, Sarah. You don't know everything. Granny Rubin sent me off to Girl Scout camp one summer. I thought I knew what to do, and I looked like a Tyrolean mountain climber. Remember last Thanksgiving you went up to Maine in some ragged clothes, and Granny Stuart sent you home in down jackets that cost two hundred dollars each, if they cost a penny? I was embarrassed. I don't want that to happen again."

I didn't say that I thought that was what grandparents were for. Mom was still uneasy about Dad's mother, who had ignored us completely until last fall when she suddenly apologized and said she'd make up for the lost years. She was sort of stiff and formal, and I guessed Cori and I would have some trouble, but a whole month's vacation in a big house on the harbor was something to look forward to. Anyway, Cleaver was going along, too. He and Crista, Granny Stuart's Bernese mountain dog, would keep her busy.

"Where are you and Dad going?" I asked, trying to make her forget about Granny Stuart.

"He won't tell me. I think I know, but I could be wrong, so I won't say anything."

"What does he have on his mind about doing when you come back?"

"That I really don't know. These Yankees, as Granny Rubin calls them, keep things to themselves. I haven't the faintest idea. But I can tell you, Sarah, that if we don't like it, we won't go along with it. You and Cori get a vote, too. We're a couple of modern women, Sarah, you and I," she laughed. "I don't know exactly what Cori is. The local crazy, I'm afraid. Look, here she comes running down the road in all this heat, Margo right behind. What do you suppose they're up to now?"

Cori and her best friend ever burst into the Good Luck. "Mom, Mom!" Cori shouted. "They're making a movie in town, a TV movie, the man said. They took pictures of our café and the stand and Margo and me and the Michaelses and the truck garden. How about that? I think they even shot the diner as they drove by. Did you see them?"

"No, I was in the kitchen."

"They didn't say they'd use it, Cori," Margo reminded her. "It's for background or local color or something. They need some pictures of a small town. The rest they are making in a studio, Dad said."

"I need your camera, Sarah," Cori demanded, without a please. "I won't break it, I promise. I want to take pictures of them taking pictures."

I hadn't taken a single picture myself with the new camera. It was automatic, Dad told me, and practically took the pictures by itself. Still, it had buttons and knobs you had to understand and you had to study the little lights that came on and you had to put in the film. I kept it under the counter and practiced when I wasn't busy. The night before, Dad brought home film and helped me load it. I wasn't about to let Cori take the first pictures. I remembered her charging me for the ice-cream cones, too. Maybe I'd never let her use it. "No way," I told her flatly.

"Do you have a camera, Mom? An old one I can borrow?"

"I never had one. Dad used to, but he dropped it. I don't believe it works at all now."

"Well, that's that, Margo. Let's get Cleaver and go to the center."

"I do have a suggestion," Mom said. "Why don't you ask Sarah to go along and take some pictures for you? Go on, Sarah, it will do you good to get out of here for a couple of hours."

Feeling foolish, I slipped my camera over my shoulder like the Japanese did. I wondered if I should have a white hat and white shorts and clean white tennis shoes.

"Come on, Sarah, if you're coming," Cori ordered. She had Cleaver on his leash. He looked confused as we turned toward town. He almost never went in that direction. He didn't recognize any of the smells. But he pricked up his ears, ready for anything that might come along.

Two men were standing in the back of a pickup truck, one on one side and one on the other, shooting the common and the sidewalk and the Congregational church and I couldn't see what else. No one was paying them any attention. There was practically no one on the sidewalk in the summer, unless it was some tourists who were lost. Most people did their shopping at the mall. The center looked deserted.

"Hey, Todd, pull over," one of the men shouted to the driver. He hopped down to talk to Todd. He had on boots, real tight jeans, and a Red Sox cap. "We're not getting anything," he told Todd. "The place is dead."

"That's your problem, Jackson," the man in the cab said. "The director told me to bring you to Stanhope, Connecticut. It's supposed to be a typical New England town." He bent over to look at some papers. "Yeah, here it is. Stanhope: The common—that's the park there—big white church, brick town hall—that must be down the street—and people on sidewalk. Move in close when something looks good. That's it. They don't need much good stuff, he said. Two minutes is the most."

"Two minutes of what? We have to have something moving besides the pickup." He saw Cori and Margo and me standing. "Hi, I saw the two of you before back at the farm, didn't I? That your dog?"

Cori nodded. Jackson didn't ask if I was Cori's big sister. I had the camera out and was trying to get it up to my eye to see if I had a good picture of the movie pickup.

The guy in the Red Sox cap came over. "Need some help? I'm Jackson. You hold it like this." He took my camera and held it up to his face. "Like this, see? This way you can shoot fast. It's an automatic. It will take pictures as fast as you want it to." Jackson looked at the camera more carefully. "Holy cow!" he exclaimed. "It's a Tonka. Look, Harris, a real live Tonka. They don't even sell them in this country."

Seeing that I was puzzled, he said, "You don't know what this is, Miss . . . What's your name?"

"I'm Sarah, her sister," I said, pointing to Cori. "What's so special about a Tonka?"

"It's the best thirty-five millimeter ever made. How come you have one? The company makes them only for Japanese millionaires. Not many, either. May I use it?"

Before I could answer, Jackson knelt and started pointing my Tonka in all directions, shooting mostly Cleaver, who had sat down, panting hard, to watch what was going on. He kept shooting Cleaver from every side until a red light flashed.

"I'll get some of my film," Jackson said. "It's quality stuff." He took out my film cartridge and gave it to me. "Where did you get this, Sarah?" he asked. "Is your father a big shot?"

I shook my head. "A Japanese man gave it to me."

"Just gave it to you, like that? Do you have any idea what one of these Tonkas goes for in Japan?"

"No."

"I don't, either, but you can bet it's a whole lot more than I'll ever have. I don't suppose you want to trade." He took a camera from his bag, sort of like mine except it was scratched up and didn't have all the gadgets. "This is a Leica. It has the best lens in the business. Well, almost the best."

"No, I can't. I'm supposed to use it to take pictures of Cleaver here to send to the man's son in Japan. The kid fell in love with our dog."

Jackson stood up. "How about that? Did you hear, Todd? The guy gave his camera away for dog pictures. Is this what Stanhope looks like all the time?"

"Yeah," said Cori.

"Dead like this?"

Cori shrugged. "I dunno, sort of like this except on the Fourth of July and town day. Slow, I guess you'd say."

Jackson gave what Cori said some thought. "Hey, Todd, how about we fill in with the kids and the dog.

We can move in and out against the street and the park here. I have to have some action."

"It's fine with me. I don't think Stillman knows what he wants. Go ahead."

"Okay, Cori, this is what we're going to do. You and your friend go over to the park and let Cleaver off his leash. Make him run or chase something. Then leash him up and cross the street and move along the sidewalk. Look in store windows. Don't pay any attention to us. Is there an ice-cream parlor in town or candy store or something?"

"Down there," Margo said. She pointed to the Bon Bon. "It's all they make."

"Great. We'll end up there. You two go in. Or one of you and leave the dog with the other guy. Here's a five-dollar bill. Harris, you take care of filming. I'm going to do some stills. I'll borrow your camera, Sarah. We'll take turns shooting Cleaver and the girls while Harris does his thing."

For about an hour Cleaver and Cori and Margo were stars. Harris told them to take their ice-cream cones back to the park. Every once in a while, Cori held Cleaver's cone out for him to take a lick. Harris seemed to like that.

Jackson gave me a handful of cartridges. "Some of these may be good. Send them to Tokyo."

"What about the movie?" Cori demanded.

"Who knows? Harris and I shoot the local color. That's our business. We give it to the director. Maybe he'll use it, maybe he won't."

"Yeah, but what's it about?"

"What's it about, Todd?"

"It's a love story about three girls who come to New York. A guy falls in love with all three. One of them is from a place like Stanhope. I hear it's a dog. No offense, Cleaver."

15

We were going to Maine on Sunday. Mom closed the diner Saturday at noon. Cori made a big sign to put in the window: CLOSED DURING AUGUST. Mom had already told all the regulars.

On Friday, Dad gave each of us an itinerary of where he and Mom were going. Mom almost fainted. She and Dad were making a tour of France and Switzerland. "Good Lord, Ed. What have you done?"

"I did better on the launderettes than I figured. Anyway, my folks used to take me to Europe in the summer. I never liked it much, because I didn't have any friends there and one old church looked like any other old church. And I didn't like the food—no hot dogs where we stayed, only fancy food. I thought I'd better take another look."

I took my copy to my room and found my fifth-grade geography book. Paris I knew and Monte Carlo, where they made a lot of movies. But places like Aix and Dijon and Avignon I hadn't heard of. At the end, a place called Bern in Switzerland. I wondered if this was Cleaver's hometown.

Mom and Dad were spending Sunday night at Granny Stuart's, coming home on Monday, and flying to Paris from New York Tuesday evening. Now Mom was bent over a big trunk laying out our clothes. Cori was complaining that she wanted her own suitcase; she didn't want to share a trunk with sister Sarah. "We have separate rooms up there, Mom. What am I supposed to do, go to Sarah's room and beg whenever I want a pair of socks? That's not fair, Mom."

"Has it occurred to you, Cori," Mom explained, "that you unpack the trunk and put *your* clothes in *your* bureau in *your* room and Sarah does the same. Then you can fight over who gets the empty trunk."

"Yeah, but who's going to pack it again?"

"Your granny Stuart doesn't know it yet, but I'm sure she is. Or I will when we come up to get you."

Cori couldn't think of anything else to fuss about. She sat on the floor and pulled Cleaver down into her lap. "What about Cleaver? We better take his extra leash and his allergy pills, in case his ear blows up."

Cleaver's ear got red and sore from time to time; he scratched dirt into the ear and it became infected. "It's an allergy," Dr. Fuller said. "It's his food or something in the ground." He gave us some pills.

Cleaver pulled away from Cori. He whined. He had been acting strange since Mom closed the diner at noon instead of when it was dark. And for two days Cori hadn't been at the Michaelses' and Cleaver couldn't go to the sit-down place. Now there were trunks and suitcases, which Cleaver hadn't seen before. He knew what knapsacks and sleeping bags were, but not suitcases. He sniffed the big trunk. He wandered out to Mom and Dad's room and sniffed the suitcases. He didn't find any suitcases in Granny Rubin's room. That seemed to bother him.

Granny Rubin was staying home. Granny Stuart had invited her and kept on inviting her, but she refused. Dad urged her, saying she needed a vacation, too. Mom was worried. "You're seventy-six years old, Mama. Come along with the girls. What if something happens here?"

"You're right, Benedicta, I'm no spring chicken. So what's going to happen? Every morning I promise to walk down to the Michaelses' to let them see I'm still alive. If I don't show up, they walk up here to see if I'm not alive. The Michaelses know where I am, they know where you are, they know where the girls are. What's the problem, Benedicta? You worry too much. Go off to Europe and enjoy yourselves."

Granny Rubin wasn't much interested in Europe. "I've been there once," she said. "And that was too much. America is good enough for Cleaver and me." She slipped Cleaver an extra prune.

Cleaver was still confused and worried Sunday morning. He ate his breakfast, but he didn't gulp it down. He kept looking over his shoulder at the rest of us as though he were disappointed in us.

"You're going to Maine, Cleaver," I told him. "You're going to see Crista. Remember Crista?"

Cleaver wasn't interested. He stood to one side when Dad lugged the trunk down the steps and out to the Toyota. He threw our sleeping bags in and Mom's overnight case. But Cleaver didn't jump in the back and tell us to hurry along, he was ready to roll. You could see he was really sad about something.

"What is it, Cleaver? You're going to Maine. How about that?" Cori said.

Cleaver pulled away. He went over to Granny Rubin who was waiting to say good-bye to us. She held out a prune. Cleaver sniffed and wouldn't take it.

"This dog is sick," she announced. "Take him to the dog doctor when you arrive. There's something wrong with him."

"Nothing's wrong with him, Granny," Dad said. "All dogs get upset when somebody leaves. Somehow they know that suitcases are trouble for them."

"That's silly," Mom said. "He was ready enough to go to Twisted Lake. In fact, he insisted. Why isn't he in the car now?"

"He doesn't understand, Nettie. I think he counted the suitcases. He couldn't find Granny Rubin's. Drag him in the car, you two. Let's take off."

Cleaver wouldn't drag. He stood like a rock next to Granny Rubin. Cori pushed and I pulled and Granny

Rubin coaxed. Cleaver rolled over and wouldn't be pushed or dragged or coaxed.

"We used to have dogs and it was awful when we went away," Dad said. "They had to go to a kennel. They could smell it five miles off. They almost tore the station wagon apart trying to escape. Come on, Cleaver. Move." He dragged Cleaver on his back. Cleaver turned over and lunged to his feet. He showed his teeth and snarled. We had never heard his snarl before.

"He's not going to leave you," Dad said to Granny Rubin. "Tell him it's okay."

"Cleaver, you stupid dog. What do you think you're doing? What's with you today? A prune?" She held out a pitted prune and walked slowly to the Toyota. Cleaver watched. He took a step or two and stopped.

"Get in the back, Mama. See what happens."

"He's more trouble than Cori," Granny Rubin grumbled. She opened the door to the backseat and climbed in the car. Cleaver leaped in beside her.

"Hurray," Dad cheered. "Now slip out and shut the door quick."

Granny climbed out and slammed the door in Cleaver's face. Cleaver jumped over the seat and out the back. We had forgotten to close that door.

"He won't fall for that again," Dad said. "Maybe if Granny Rubin put a suitcase of hers in, it might work."

"Good idea," Mom said. "Don't you bother, Mama. I'll take care of it. We can't spend all day on Cleaver's problems."

Mom took a long time. "What are you doing, Nettie?" Dad shouted up the steps.

"I have to throw some clothes in it, don't I, Ed? You don't think the dog is going to be fooled by an empty suitcase."

Mom took some more time. Cori and I were itching to leave. Dad, too. Granny Rubin kept on scolding Cleaver for being a troublemaker.

Mom came out at last. She put the suitcase in front of Cleaver for him to sniff. "Come along, Mama," she said. She shoved the suitcase in the back and opened the side door. Granny Rubin climbed in. Cleaver jumped in. He leaned over to slurp Granny Rubin. Dad shut the back door. Mom shut the side door.

"Don't let either one of them out," she ordered. "I have to close the windows and lock the doors in the house. I'll be right back."

Dad told Cori and me to climb in next to Granny Rubin. He guarded the door. Cleaver curled up in the tiny space left by the trunk and suitcases and sleeping bags. Mom got in the front seat. "Let's go, Ed," she ordered.

It took a while for Granny Rubin to realize what had happened. We expected her to holler and bang on the door, but she settled back and dropped a prune on top of Cleaver, who gobbled it down. She put her arm around me. "Someone has to go along to look after that crazy Cleaver," she said.

—16—

When we arrived in Castine, Maine, Cleaver forgot about Granny Rubin and the rest of us. He began to whine and paw the car door as soon as he had a sniff of the sea. The minute Dad parked in the Stuart driveway and lifted up the back door, Cleaver shot to the ground. He couldn't figure out which way to head, across the road and down to the harbor, where he had a swim last Thanksgiving, or to the front door of the big, white house, which we could scarcely see now that the two sugar maples in the front yard had all their leaves.

"Humph," Granny Rubin snorted, easing herself out of the Toyota. "He can't make his mind up between his girlfriend and a swim in the ocean. If he's like most men, he'll head for the water. I'll bet you twenty-five cents on the ocean, Sarah."

Cleaver looked at Dad for help in making up his mind. He didn't get any help from Dad, so he headed for the ocean.

95

"Cleaver," Dad snapped. "No road." He grabbed Cleaver's collar and led him to the curb. "No road. Sit. Get me his leash, Cori." He snapped on the leash and led Cleaver across the road. "Sit," he ordered. "No road," he reminded him, and led him back to the Toyota where he took off the leash. Cleaver headed to the front door.

"Twenty-five cents, Granny Rubin," I held out my hand.

"He headed for the ocean, the stupid dog. I won," she replied. "He just didn't make it."

"Yeah, but look where he is now, at the front door waiting for Crista. I won."

"It's a tie," Dad said. "Help me get the luggage out."

The front door swung open and Cleaver dashed in. Granny Stuart looked after him, laughed, and came toward the car. She hugged Mom and Granny Rubin, a sort of formal hug, and gave her only son, Edward, a motherly hug. "A hug or a handshake?" she asked Cori.

"A hug, I guess," Cori said, and put her arms around Granny Stuart's neck. A long time ago, Cori figured out that was the easiest way to get along with family.

It was harder for me. I *wanted* to hug Granny Stuart, but I couldn't. I put my hand out. Granny Stuart took it firmly. "You're too big for all this hugging business, aren't you, Sarah? So was I all my life, even with Edward, but in the last year I seem to have taken it up. It helps break the ice."

Mom and Dad were carrying in luggage and oohing

and aahing over how great the house and lawn looked, trying to get over their embarrassment. Cori had disappeared inside to check on Cleaver and Crista.

Cori ran back down the steps to the front door. "It's a lot bigger," she announced. "Lots of new bathrooms and things. Up in the attic, too. It's not the same at all. What's going on?" she asked Granny Stuart.

Granny Stuart frowned a little. You could see that Cori had stolen her thunder. She wasn't used to having kids around. She was going to have trouble with Cori, I knew right away.

Mom gave Cori a real tough look. She bent over to whisper, "You be quiet from now on . . ." She couldn't figure out the "or else." She was going away and Granny Rubin let Corinthia get away with murder. "Or else," she said, just "or else."

Cori looked ashamed of herself the way she always did when someone rebuked her. "Sorry, Mom," she whispered. She moved out of sight.

The upstairs was different. Some of the big rooms were smaller rooms now. The huge attic was now three rooms with sloping ceilings and window seats at large windows facing the harbor. And there was a whole new section out back with a sun room and an outdoor deck. Bathrooms everywhere, too. What was going on? It wasn't the same house at all we had visited last Thanksgiving. I wasn't sure I liked the new old house; it didn't look as comfortable. Granny Stuart had said something about bringing our friends with us, but Cori and I didn't have that many friends who could spend part of their summers in Castine. Cori had Margo, but she had to work at the farm, and I, well, I couldn't think of a soul. I had a feeling that something else was going on, like Mom and Dad's trip to Europe. It was something funny, and I started to worry, again. I realized I didn't like change.

"This was an old sea captain's house," Granny Stuart was explaining to Mom and Granny Rubin. "It was fine for me, but uncomfortable until you were accustomed to it. So, I got in an architect and told him what I wanted—a usable big house for a big family. This is what he did. It will be easier to sell, anyway. Now, I'll show you where to stay tonight."

I had a room with a bath between my room and another one. Cori had a bigger room with her own bath, just like Granny Rubin's at the other end of the hall.

"There are some changes in the back of the house, too," Granny Stuart said. She led us down the steps. Cori was coming up the steps lickety split, followed only by Crista, Cleaver's sister. "Hey!" Cori shouted, "Guess what's out back!"

Granny Stuart stopped. Dad and Mom, Granny Rubin, too, stared hard at Cori.

"Yes, Cori," Granny Stuart said coldly, "What's out back?"

"Nothing," Cori put her head down, "nothing much."

Out in the backyard, which I didn't remember seeing when we were visiting last November, was a swimming pool. A big head was moving around in circles in the middle of the pool. It was Cleaver, who was looking for someone to join him.

"Well," Granny Stuart sniffed. "I should have told you, I suppose. I don't allow Crista in the pool. You will have to explain that to Cleaver."

Mom and Dad bent over the edge to explain it, but Cleaver paid no attention. He kept on paddling around in a circle.

Cori raised her hand. "Granny Stuart?" she asked.

"Yes, Corinthia?"

"Could I tell everyone it's a heated pool?"

"Please do."

"It's a heated pool, everyone. It's warm like the bathtub. I put my foot in, see? But I forgot to take my shoe off."

—*17*—

"Don't you two give your grandmother any trouble," Mom told Cori and me. Mostly she meant Cori. Mom called me her quiet daughter. "Keep to your diet, Sarah. I think you've lost ten pounds or more already. And you, Mama, take your nap every afternoon."

That made Granny Rubin mad. She didn't like her daughter telling her what to do in public. "And I'll brush my teeth, too, Benedicta. Watch over her, Ed. She's never been away from home before. Humph."

Dad backed the Toyota out the road and turned toward home. He and Mom waved and the car disappeared around a turn. For some reason Cori and I started to cry at the same time. We would be alone for only the second time we could remember without Mom to look after us, and it would be a whole month. Cori wiped her sniffles on her sleeve. She pulled at my hand. "Let's go swimming in the pool. Last one in is a rotten egg." Leaving the rest of them on the lawn, Cori and I ran up the steps to change.

That was about the last good day we saw for a while. Low clouds moved in to hang over Castine and a cool, damp breeze blew from over the harbor. We still went swimming, but it wasn't much fun without sunshine. As soon as you climbed out of the pool you got goose bumps.

"It's like this some Augusts," Granny Stuart told us. "The cold air and the warm are mixed up. It will clear after a while."

The sky did clear some mornings and we took Crista and Cleaver to the little beach by the boat yard, sometimes with a picnic basket, but usually a cold mist rolled in and we dragged the dogs home. We discovered that television in Maine wasn't like television in Stanhope. Granny Stuart had forgotten to put in cable when it came around, and we were stuck with three fuzzy pictures, one of them in French.

Granny Stuart had our schedule all laid out, including Granny Rubin's and Cleaver's. It was typed up and tacked to the bulletin board in the brand-new all-stainless-steel kitchen. Cori read to Cleaver what he was supposed to do. "Up at seven, Cleaver," she told him, "and outside to go to the bathroom. No pool, do you hear? No pool ever for you. Do you suppose we have to take him out to the yard on his leash, Sarah?"

"We'll take turns," I replied.

"What a vacation," Cori grumbled. "Then inside for your breakfast, Cleaver," she went on. "Nap in dog room until walk time. You can swim in the harbor if you want. Back to dog room. A light supper at six—what do you suppose a light supper is, Sarah?—and out to use the bathroom. Then off to bed. Did you hear that, Cleaver?"

Cleaver hadn't been listening, I could see. As soon as Cori let go of his collar, he headed upstairs to check the wastebaskets. Cleaver liked to chew on paper tissues and towels. At home we had to empty the wastebaskets twice a day. The very first day we were there, Granny Stuart caught him in her room, his head in her wastebasket. She spoke sharply at him and he crept downstairs, tail between his legs, looking ashamed—a scented blue tissue in his mouth.

For Granny Rubin, once she got used to the house, Granny Stuart had a really big project, a homemade quilt for Mom and Dad's bed—the one in Castine. Granny Stuart had been collecting patches of "absolutely stunning" cloth for ten years or so with a mind to making a quilt. She was just now getting around to it, she explained to Granny Rubin. They could work on it together for the next month. It would keep them out of mischief, she said. "You must have made quilts in Germany," she remarked. Granny Rubin didn't answer yes or no.

And for me, I discovered, Granny Stuart had dug up a friend, Muffy Forsythe. The Forsythes had been coming up to Castine every summer for twenty years, Granny Stuart confided. They had a house down the street. Muffy's brother Nick was at Yale in Connecticut I was told, as if I didn't know where Yale was. He worked in the restaurant on the wharf. The big news was that

Nick's sister Muffy was here for the summer, too, and free to be my friend. In the winter Muffy went to Rock Hall, a boarding school for girls up the coast a ways.

That left Cori, who didn't take up much room on the schedule, mostly question marks. Tennis lessons? Learning to sail? Trip to Quebec in third week with everyone? Muffy? "What else?" I heard Granny Stuart ask Granny Rubin, who assured her that Cori would find something to do, although it would be mostly trouble.

But then bad weather set in and Cori began to mope around the house. She took Cleaver and Crista for walks in the direction of the soft-ice-cream parlor. Granny Rubin played canasta with her and taught her to play solitaire, but by the fourth day, Cori began to yearn for her friend Margo.

"Why don't you call her up?" Granny Stuart said. "I bet she misses you, too."

"Can I?" Cori shouted. "Oh, boy! I can tell her about the pool and the soft ice cream."

Calling Margo wasn't such a hot idea. Poor Cori, I really did feel sorry for her. Margo had been so upset losing her best friend ever that the Michaelses had to ship her off to her grandparents for a while to a little summer cabin on a pond with mosquitoes and no kids Margo's age. Mrs. Michaels promised Cori she would tell Margo all about the pool and the soft-ice-cream stand.

—18—

The bad weather forced Granny Stuart to revise the schedule. She decided that we would all go to Quebec during the bad weather. She hadn't been there for years. Granny Rubin politely declined. She would look after Crista and Cleaver and study the patches of cloth for the quilt. That would leave room for Muffy Forsythe, Granny Stuart said. Sarah and Muffy could get acquainted in the back while she and Cori could have some good talks up front. Cori rolled her eyes and stuck out her tongue behind Granny Stuart's back.

Muffy turned out to be a tall, blond fifteen-year-old in her second year at the Rock Hall Academy. She came by the afternoon before the big trip to meet Cori and me and Granny Rubin. As soon as I saw her I began to feel fat and shabby all over. We shook hands and went out to meet Cleaver in the dog room. Cleaver raised his head to see if the stranger had a handout. When nothing happened, he sighed and shut his eyes. "He looks like a nice dog," Muffy told Cori and me. "We have a cat, Tabby. Samantha is what Mother calls her. She has short hair. Mother is allergic to long-haired cats." Muffy had heard all about Quebec in her French course at Rock Hall.

"It is part of France, spiritually," she declared. "On the license plates of their cars, it says *Je me souviens*. That means, 'I will remember I am French.' French people there are very proud of being French."

I said something about how I thought they were Canadian. Muffy told me that was so, but they really wanted to be French. That was why they didn't like to speak English. She was looking forward to practicing her French on the trip.

Cori took a sharp interest in the conversation. "Don't be dumb, Sarah. It's like Cleaver is Swiss although he lives in Connecticut.

"My grandparents came from Germany," she told Muffy proudly. "I don't know where my other grandparents came from. What I mean is, I don't know where my Stuart grandparents came from."

Granny Stuart explained that the Stuarts came from Scotland and her folks, the Hootens, were Dutch once upon a time.

"Mom said you were a Yankee," Cori piped up. "What does that mean?"

"I think it means someone who lives in this part of the world. I hope that's what your mother meant, anyway. I have new knapsacks which should be enough for you girls to take your clothes in, red for Sarah and a green for you, Corinthia."

"Is it all right if Sarah and I trade? Red is my favorite color and Sarah doesn't care. Do you, Sarah?"

That didn't sit so well with Granny Stuart. She liked things the way that she decided they should be. That meant red for Sarah and green for Cori. "Well, if you have to, Corinthia, I suppose it's all right. I rather had it in my head you were a green girl."

"Nope, red," Cori said happily, and grabbed my red knapsack.

Cori was allowed to have the red knapsack, but not rock music on the car radio. When we set off, Muffy and I took the backseat of the big American car, leaving Cori up in the front seat with our grandmother, which was all right with Cori because there were more buttons and knobs on the front panel for her to fiddle with than you could count. First, Cori turned on the air conditioner, which Granny Stuart told her we didn't need because it was already chilly outside. Next the automatic windows, which Granny Stuart told Cori the driver was in charge of. Last of all, Cori turned on the stereophonic radio. The music nearly blasted us out of the backseat because the speakers were placed right at our ears.

"Really, Corinthia," Granny Stuart said. "I don't think I can take it. Does your mother let you play the car radio that loud and listen to such dreadful music, if that's what they call it?"

106

"The Toyota doesn't have a radio. We have to carry our little portables." Cori snapped off the radio and slumped in the corner of her seat.

Granny Stuart sighed. "Are you two girls all right back there?"

"We're fine," I reassured her.

When Muffy saw the hotel where we were staying, she told me it was like a Norman castle. And the old city sitting on top of the hill looking over the St. Lawrence River was just like a town in Brittany. "I am going to Switzerland next summer to a camp my mother went to," she said. "Maine is a drag year-round."

As soon as we checked in, Granny Stuart told us we would start on a tour of the city. "I'm going to stay here," Cori stated. "I'll be all right." She turned on the big television set in the room she was sharing with Granny Stuart. Some man was talking in French. The next station was playing an old American sitcom except the actors weren't speaking English. Another station was talking in English about codfish. Cori snapped off the set. "I'm ready," she told us.

Cori needed some help, so when Granny Stuart started walking beside Muffy to practice her French, I drifted back to be with Cori. "What's the matter?" I asked.

Cori didn't give me a smart answer. "I dunno. It's not as much fun as I thought it would be—sort of like the carnival. It's not what I thought it would be."

"It's because you don't have any friends, isn't it?

107

Maybe you could ask Granny Stuart to invite Margo up the last two weeks."

"It's not only that," Cori said. "I feel strange, sort of out of place. I miss Mom and the diner, not just Margo. I'm not sure I like Granny Stuart. I can't fight back with Granny Stuart the way I fight with Mom and Dad and Granny Rubin."

"You never fight with Granny Rubin," I pointed out. "She always gives in."

"I know, but I could if I wanted to."

Cori and I hung pretty close the next two days. Muffy was happy to be talking French with Granny Stuart about Rock Hall and the summer people who came to Castine. The meals didn't help, either. Granny Stuart told us at least half a dozen times the restaurants in Quebec were famous for their French cooking and we should be open-minded about ordering. Cori and I honestly tried, but like Quebec television, there was nothing much there for us. I was glad I could say I was on a diet. Granny Stuart sighed a lot, and it seemed to me Muffy sighed, too, being in the company of such nerds as Cori and me.

19

Cleaver had taken to snoozing beside Granny Rubin's rocking chair in the living room while we were in Canada. He knew he wasn't supposed to be there but the dog room was on the other side of the pantry, which was on the other side of the kitchen, two rooms away from the kitchen where the good smells were and four rooms away from people. Crista had her balsam pad and stayed in the dog room where she should when she wasn't outside. Cleaver had a brand-new pad all his own in the dog room, but he didn't like to stay put. There wasn't any action in the dog room.

Cleaver lifted his head when we arrived late in the afternoon. He put his head down between his paws and stared at Granny Stuart. Granny Stuart paused for a moment to stare back. She then carried her bag up the steps. Granny Rubin came back to her rocker. She looked down at Cleaver as though she just found out he was there. "What are you doing in here, Cleaver?

Don't you know where your place is?" Cleaver didn't pay any attention.

"Cori," Granny Rubin whispered. "Get him out to the dog room. Or take him outside. Here." She handed Cori a couple of prunes. Cleaver pulled himself together and I followed after Cori out to the dog room. "You stay out there and lose weight," she told him.

Cleaver didn't see it that way. He went straight through the dog room to the back door and stood there impatiently, wanting to go out. Crista watched, then she decided she wanted out, too. Cori opened the door. Cleaver pounded past, Crista close behind. It looked like they were playing rotten egg, both of them hitting the water about the same time. "Hey, Sarah," Cori exclaimed. "Isn't that cute? Maybe we could teach them to have a swimming race."

After a good swim, Cleaver put his paws on the edge of the pool and whined to get out. I took his front paws and pulled him out; Cori did the same for Crista. They shook all over Cori and me and headed for the back door. Inside, all the doors were open to the parlor where the two grannies were kneeling over the quilt. Crista and Cleaver had a second shake in the middle of the quilt.

Granny Stuart glared at Cori and Me. "That's it," she snapped. "Dogs in dog room. Outside, dogs on leash. I'm sorry," she mumbled to Granny Rubin. "Crista must be a bad influence on your dog."

"Did you hear that, you two?" Granny Rubin snapped.

She was talking to Cori and me, not the dogs. "Dogs in dog room."

We came back with kitchen towels to wipe up. Granny Rubin was explaining about Bernese mountain dogs to Granny Stuart. She had listened to Dad talk about them enough to tell Granny Stuart that they were people dogs. "They have to be around a family, Alice, sometimes. Cleaver worries about us."

"I haven't noticed Crista worrying about me," Granny Stuart sniffed. "All she does is sleep in the dog room."

"You should give her snacks," Granny Rubin said. "Then she will worry."

Granny Rubin whispered to me later that she had let Cleaver have the full run of the house at night while we were in Quebec in case of bad guys. When Cori and I tricked him into the dog room that evening after his walk, Cleaver insisted that his place was no longer in the dog room at night. At home he slept in the kitchen but we left the door into the rest of the house open at night so Cleaver could make his rounds once or twice to see if everyone was all right. You wouldn't hear him sniffing around in the upstairs hall, but when he went down the steps it was a *thump-thump-thump* that made the house shake.

No sooner had we gone to bed than Cleaver let loose with an unhappy whine. I heard Cori go down to tell him to shut up. Ten minutes later, Cleaver started up again. By then Cori was asleep. Granny Stuart was the next one to explain the rules to Cleaver. I was pretty

111

sure she was saying something like, "Look at Crista." Cleaver remembered his place as a guest and shut up. Later that night, however, he realized it was time to make his rounds and moaned and barked. Cori crept down and opened the door to the dog room and went back up to bed.

Cleaver was quiet enough until he went down the steps after he checked up on everyone. The thumps woke Granny Stuart up. She thought maybe it was a burglar, so she went downstairs to find Cleaver sleeping on his back beside Granny Rubin's rocker. Crista was there with him.

At breakfast, she laid down the law again. Dogs in the dog room at night was the message. "That's right," Granny Rubin echoed.

"Cleaver sleeps in our kitchen with the door open at home," Cori talked back.

"Well, he shouldn't do that," Granny Rubin said.

"You're the one who lets him," Cori said.

"I know that I shouldn't. When we go home, I'll ask your father to make him a nice doghouse."

"We'll see about that," Cori said. "Cleaver will sleep in *my* room if he wants to."

Granny Stuart listened to them argue, shaking her head in disbelief. Dad must not have been brought up to talk back to Granny Stuart.

—20—

The next day the sun broke through the clouds that had been hanging over Castine for a week. Granny Stuart stood in the front door peering at the horizon. "Well," she declared. "We will have good weather for a while, perhaps for the rest of the month. I'll give Muffy a call."

"I have a surprise for you," Granny Stuart announced, while we waited for Muffy to show up. "I rented a small sailboat from the boatyard. Muffy will teach you how to sail. If the weather holds true, you might be good enough to show off to your father when he comes to fetch you. Muffy is a first-rate sailor. She and Nick were first at the junior regatta last summer."

Granny Stuart must have noticed that Cori and I were not jumping with joy. She looked worried. "Is something wrong? I haven't done the wrong thing again, have I?"

"No," I tried to explain. "It's not that. It's just that the harbor looks pretty big and rough for us. I guess we're a little bit scared."

"And Dad said *his* dad, who was a super sailor, drowned out there when Dad was growing up. He was my grandfather," Cori joined in. I couldn't kick her, but I looked daggers.

"Your father is right," Granny Stuart agreed. "David was being careless. He always refused to wear his life jacket. There is a strong tide in the harbor. David's boat tipped over and he tried to swim ashore against the tide. He knew better than that. He had a heart attack and, well, that was that."

I asked what about us, but Granny Stuart went on to tell us that we would learn about sailing at the little beach next to the wharf. We would wear our life jackets at all times and if we went outside it would be a on a calm day when the tide was right and Nick and Muffy would be in charge and only one of us at a time. I could see that didn't sound like much fun to Cori. She made a face behind Granny Stuart's back. Cori liked to do things her own way.

Cori was right. It wasn't much fun learning about the sails and the rigging and the mast and the boom and the rudder on a sailboat anchored in two feet of water. Muffy was a bossy teacher and didn't even bother to answer Cori when she butted in the fourth time or so to ask one of her dumb questions. Toward the end of the second lesson Cori gave up and sat on the wharf watching Muffy and me. On the third day she brought Cleaver along—in spite of Granny Stuart's objections that Cleaver probably didn't want to be a sailor—and threw a stick out in the water for him to fetch. Cleaver came up to the boat to see what was going on, and Muffy told him he didn't want to be a sailor. It struck me that Muffy and Granny Stuart were sort of the same, remote and superior. Sometimes they even forgot their good manners.

That evening Cori told me she wanted to go home. She wanted me to call up Margo's father and ask if Margo was back and did they have room for Cori for the rest of the month. "You can think up a better reason for me to leave than I can, Sarah," she begged me.

"I can't do that, Cori," I explained. "Granny Rubin won't let you go. Do you think I like it here any better than you do? I'd almost rather be working in the diner. We have to stick it out until Mom and Dad come back. You're just lonely, that's all. Granny Stuart is all right. She's not used to having kids around."

"Dogs, either," Cori answered.

The next day when Nick came by with Muffy in his Jeep with balloon tires to take us for a visit to Muffy's school, Cori said she wasn't feeling well and would stay home. Cleaver was feeling fine and tried to squeeze into the backseat with me until Granny Stuart grabbed his collar. "You have to stay home with Corinthia," she told him.

Rock Hall Academy used to be a summer place a rich New York family sailed up to in their yacht, Muffy explained. It was a bore most of the time, she complained, but her mother had gone to Rock Hall along with lots of her friends, so Muffy had to go there now along with the daughters of her mother's friends.

The wind blew in from the ocean, and when clouds swept over the sun, the school looked like a reformatory. It was a big rock building with a bunch of smaller rock-and-board cabins which used to be for the rich guy's guests. The school ran a summer sailing camp, and the students all seemed to know Nick and Muffy. They squealed and hugged Muffy and talked to Nick in grown-up accents. I was glad Cori hadn't come. She would have felt even more out of place than I did.

"It's not so bad when you get used to it," Muffy said. "We have indoor tennis courts and horses and a winter program in Switzerland for six weeks where you can ski."

All I could think of to say was, "That's neat."

"Why don't you tell her it's a prison?" Nick laughed.

"It's a lot better school than that preppy place you went to," Muffy replied. "I don't think you learned anything there. You'd like it here, Sarah, I think."

"Me?"

"That's what Alice said. She asked me to bring you over. Don't you go to high school the year after next? They might let you bring your dog. A couple of the girls have their dogs here—but they are little poodles and terriers. Maybe they wouldn't take a big dog."

"My grandmother said I might be coming here?" I asked in disbelief. What was Granny Stuart thinking of? I'd leave school before I'd go to Rock Hall.

"Sort of. I think your father told her you weren't doing so well in school, and the high school where you live is pretty bad. That gave Alice the idea, I guess."

"She hasn't said anything to me," I replied. "I'll ask her about it. It was nice of you to bring me over." No big dogs, Muffy had said, so I added, "I don't think I could come without Cleaver."

Muffy and Nick headed for the Jeep. I could swear I heard my new friend Muffy say, "Suit yourself."

—21—

Nick dumped me off at Granny Stuart's front door. "See you around, Sarah," he said. Behind Muffy's back, he rolled his eyes at his sister. Nick wasn't so bad. Muffy sort of nodded and leaned forward so I could ease myself out of the Jeep. What was I going to tell Granny Stuart about my trip to the Rock Hall Academy? I wondered if Mom knew anything about what was going on. She had probably said something to Dad who had said something to his mother who took it into her head that Rock Hall was just the place for her granddaughter. Other grannies must be sending their granddaughters there.

Or was something else going on? It seemed to Cori and me that Granny Stuart was being extra careful about how she talked to us sometimes, like she was collecting her thoughts before she said this or that. Except when she was having trouble with Cleaver. She was pretty definite about how he should behave and where his place was.

I didn't have to explain about Muffy and the trip to Rock Hall. Granny Stuart held the door open for me and ordered me inside. She was pale and her face was twitching. Granny Rubin was standing next to Mr. Tuttle, who ran the boatyard and was the harbormaster. Cori was sitting on the second step of the staircase, her arms around her knees, and looking down at her bare feet. Her clothes were wet. In the side parlor I saw Cleaver on the antique quilt licking himself dry. Crista was right beside him. She was dry.

Mr. Tuttle gave me a little nod. "As I was saying, Alice, I was watching the girl here, wondering where Alison— I guess they call her Muffy, Lord knows why—and Sarah were. She had her dog with her. She beached the boat and went through the training routine. Pretty good at it, I'd say." Mr. Tuttle smiled at Cori.

"She sat there for a while fiddling with the boom. She called to the dog and he jumped in the boat. She pretended she was sailing the boat. Then a gust of wind came down the hill and blew the boat off the beach. The girl here—Cori's her name, right?—grabbed the rudder and she sailed away from the pilings nice as you please. Where did you think you were going, Cori?"

Cori lifted her head. "I don't know. I just didn't want to smash into the wharf. Muffy and Granny Stuart would really be mad with me then." She cast her eyes down on her feet again. Granny Stuart started to cry. She sat down on the step next to Cori and hugged her tight.

"She took it outside like a real sailor," Mr. Tuttle went on. "She had me fooled for a moment. Right out to the middle of the harbor. Another big gust came down, stronger this time, and the boat went over, dumping Cori here and the dog into the water. The tide grabbed the boat and pulled it away. That's when I jumped into my dinghy and got it started.

"The dog swam in circles around Cori until she grabbed him by the collar. Then he took off for the shore, swimming with the tide. Did you tell him to do that, Cori?"

Cori shook her head. "That's just what he did," she murmured.

"That was the right thing, too. He's a real smart dog. By the time I got to them he was halfway to the light-house and still going strong. I reckon he would have made it without any trouble."

"Thank you for coming after us," Cori said. "I'm sorry I caused the trouble."

"No trouble at all. Glad I was there. Though you and your dog didn't need me. I'll go get my boat back." Mr. Tuttle looked at his watch. "The tide's about to change, anyway. No trouble there, either. You take care of her, Alice. You got yourself a good one there. No need to tell Ed, I'd say. It might worry him." Mr. Tuttle reached down to rub Cori's wet head and left.

Granny Stuart never said a word about Cori's adventure. After that she didn't chase Cleaver and Crista off the antique quilt, either. She decided to work around them.

But Granny Rubin pretended to care, for appearance's sake. "Get off there," she said to Cleaver. "Here—this piece is for you," she said, giving Cleaver a piece of red velvet. "And one for you, too, Crista." She told me to take them to the kitchen and give them a couple of prunes. "Ed was wrong," she said. "He's not a mountain dog, after all. Cleaver is a water dog."

—22—

After that, Granny Stuart couldn't do enough to make Cori feel happy. She got on the phone to the Michaelses to see if Margo was home. She asked them to put her on the bus to Portland, and two days later she and Cori drove down to pick Margo up.

Cori liked to brag to Margo about her adventure at the harbor. Granny Rubin took about three days of the boasting. Then one afternoon she told Cori to come upstairs with her. When Margo trailed behind to see what was going on, Granny Rubin asked her—told her, really—to stay downstairs, because she and Cori had to have a private talk.

It was a different Cori who came back downstairs to the Monopoly board. "What did she want?" I asked. Cori shook her head. She was so distracted, she let me land on Boardwalk with its two hotels without collecting about half a million dollars in rent.

Granny Rubin didn't dump on Cleaver, but she let him know that he shouldn't have let Cori go. When Granny Stuart wasn't around, she coaxed Cleaver out to the dog room. "This is your place, Cleaver," she told him sharply, shoving him down on his pad. "Stay!" No prune or anything, just "Stay!" Cleaver looked mournful and whined when Granny Rubin left, but he stayed. Crista crawled over to comfort him. Granny Stuart found him asleep in the dog room, his nose resting on Crista's back. "At last," she said, and brought them each a couple of dog yummies.

After whatever Granny Rubin said, it wasn't the same Cori. She was the first to help out in the kitchen, the first to go to bed, the first not to cheat at Monopoly, and, above all, the first not to talk back. Granny Stuart began to relax and smile a lot more. She told us how nice it was to have us around and next summer we could bring our friends for the whole time if we wanted to.

The only problem was Muffy. She came by the next day to tell Granny Stuart that Mr. Tuttle had brought the sailboat back in good condition and did we want to keep up with the lessons.

"What about it, Sarah?" Granny Stuart asked.

"We better not," I said. "We don't have any place to sail at home."

"Well, if you . . ." Granny Stuart began to say something and stopped. "Tennis, maybe. You're good at tennis, aren't you, Muffy?"

"Pretty good," Muffy agreed.

"I guess not, thank you."

Granny Stuart gave me one of her disapproving looks. "Swimming?"

"I already know how to swim," I said. I had to say something to be polite. My eyes lit on Granny Rubin bending over the quilt sewing a patch in place. "I'd like to learn quilting," I blurted out. "Is there room for me?"

Granny Stuart beamed with pleasure. "Of course there is. It's really a lot of fun when you get into it. How about you, Muffy? We have one more side."

"I'm no good at sewing," Muffy admitted. "I'll see you around, Sarah."

"How about supper some night? On the grill by the pool?" Granny Stuart called after the departing Muffy.

"Maybe," Muffy responded.

"You lost your friend, did you, Sarah?" Granny Rubin asked when I knelt beside her to see how you made a quilt.

"She wasn't really my friend."

"Don't let it bother you," Granny Rubin advised. "Enjoy yourself. How much weight have you lost? You look thinner."

"A lot, I think. There aren't any scales in the house. But I worry about it."

"You're like your mother more and more," Granny Rubin sighed.

"What's wrong with that?"

"Nothing. It's just that you look like her more every day and you worry about things the way she does. You

124

don't see Cori worrying, do you? Ed doesn't worry either. You and your sister are completely different. That's good. You'll need each other someday."

I had heard this before, but I thought a lot about what Granny Rubin said. She was right. I worried about things more than I talked about them. Maybe that was why I didn't have any close friends at school. Helen Yeng was the only girl I was close to. She was a worrier, too. I wondered about Gilberto. He looked like a worrier, but then he had more to worry about than Helen and me—like getting shot if he went home. I began to hope he was still there when we got back to Stanhope.

The three of us made great progress with the quilt. Another summer, Granny Stuart said, and we'd be finished. She promised not to work on it until Granny Rubin and I were around. She seemed pretty confident we'd all be back. She didn't talk about next summer with an "if you come back" but a "when you come back." And once she said something like "if not before."

In the afternoons between swimming and supper I slipped up to the attic where Granny Stuart had put in some bedrooms during the winter. You could see out across the harbor and down the coast beyond the old lighthouse they didn't use anymore. It was beautiful. But even with the harbor full of sailboats, it was lonely. I shivered and tried to write a chapter for Mrs. Porter about living always in sight of gray, dangerous waters and hard, brown rocks along the shore and evergreens that were too dark to comfort you. I discovered I had a lot to write about which wasn't always about Cori or Cleaver or Mom and Dad. I felt pretty comfortable writing about myself. I wasn't sure whether Mrs. Porter would think that was good or bad; I had a feeling I was doing it right.

—23—

Cleaver not only understood when people were going away but also when they were coming back. Two days before Mom and Dad returned from France, Cleaver left the parlor where he kept an eye on our progress with the quilt and took up a position by the front door. In a little while Crista joined him. "Look at that ungrateful dog," Granny Rubin said. "I let him out of the dog room to keep us company and there he is over at the door."

"He's a family dog," I told her. "He knows the rest of the family is coming back."

"Hah!" Granny Rubin exclaimed. "He thinks Benedicta is bringing him some fancy French food. Psst, Cleaver!" She held out a prune.

Cleaver took a sniff and climbed to his feet. His limp was a lot better, I noticed, and he had lost some weight. Cleaver and I, Granny Rubin remarked every day, looked a lot better since she took charge of our weight problems. Cleaver took the prune back to his place by the door and put it between his paws. He licked it a couple of times before he chewed it.

"Look at that, would you? He doesn't even want his prune. He took it to be polite," Granny Rubin grumped.

On the day before Mom and Dad showed up, Muffy came to the front door. Cleaver growled under his breath. At first I thought he was growling at Muffy, but when I held the door for her to come in, I saw she had a fluffy little black-and-white kitten in her arms. Muffy said hi and asked to speak to Alice.

"My mother wondered if you could look after Chanel for a little while," Muffy said, holding the kitten out for Granny Stuart to take.

Granny Stuart didn't immediately grab Chanel. "What gave your mother that idea?" she asked.

"She's allergic to long-haired cats, and we're closing up for the season. It's just until I come back to school. Then I'll take Chanel to Rock Hall."

Crista reached up to smell the kitten. She gave it a lick and slumped back to the floor.

"Oh, I suppose," Granny Stuart said. She took the kitten. By supper time Chanel was purring in Granny Stuart's lap. "She *is* cute," she decided.

The day Mom and Dad were to show up I felt fearful and insecure. Like Cleaver, I sensed something funny was going on. I remembered that Dad had said we were going to do something different if we all agreed. First he had to talk it over with Mom, then with the rest of us. We had lots of postcards, Cori and I, from funny-sounding places, but they didn't tell us about the big news. By afternoon I decided I didn't want to hear about it. It was bound to be bad.

"What's the matter with you, Sarah?" Granny Rubin asked. "You act like you have to go to the dentist. Can't you wait?"

"It's not that. At least that's not all of it."

"Is it because you're going back to school? Your mother always felt a little upset in the stomach the first day or two of school. You'll do better this year. You've been writing more stories, haven't you?"

I hadn't told anyone. Up on the third floor I had written four and a half stories, one about Cleaver, one about Cori's accident, and almost two and a half about me. "How did you know?" I asked Granny Rubin.

"I'm not blind, Sarah. Your mind is somewhere else, and you have been upstairs a lot. Are you thinking about rock stars, maybe?"

I shook my head. "No, I've been doing some stories for Mrs. Porter."

"Good. You will be a famous writer someday."

"I don't think so. Will I, Cleaver?"

The family dog got up, turned around once, looked out the screen door, and collapsed next to Crista, his eyes on the driveway, waiting. I sat beside him. He licked my hand to tell me he appreciated the attention and went back to watching for Mom and Dad.

When the Toyota pulled into the driveway, Cleaver

grabbed his piece of velvet and shoved his nose into the door. It was latched. He shoved harder. When that didn't work he pushed his head against the screen. It began to give. He poked his head through, then the rest of him. He roared across the lawn and circled around Mom and Dad once or twice. Mom knelt down. Cleaver climbed into her lap. She went over backward, Cleaver on top. He sprawled beside her, licking her face. Granny Stuart and Crista examined the big hole in the front screen door. "Why don't you ever do that for me, Crista?" Granny Stuart asked.

It was a tight fit in the Toyota the next morning. Granny Rubin and I sat in back, and Margo and Cori got in the wayback with Cleaver and all the stuff. Granny Stuart waited to say good-bye; Chanel cuddled in her arms. Crista was watching, not doing anything, just watching. If we had been paying attention, we would have seen that she was thinking. Cleaver did that sometimes before he moved. As Dad reached up to pull the car door down, Crista moved. In three jumps she nosed under the door and slipped into the back.

Cori and Margo squealed, then screamed as Crista settled on top of them. Cleaver tried to move over, but there wasn't room. Dad reached in to grab Crista's collar. Crista growled. Dad looked at his mother. She spoke sharply and gave Dad the cat to hold. She reached in to drag Crista out. Crista growled. Cleaver growled. Granny Stuart looked at Dad. Without a word, he gave Chanel back to Granny Stuart. He pulled the car door down.

Inside, he stuck his head out to tell Granny Stuart she was a cat person, not a dog person, and we'd bring Crista back to visit from time to time.

The house on the hill smelled damp and stale inside. It smelled like Cleaver in almost every room. Mom hurried around throwing open the windows while Dad and I brought in the suitcases. Cori took off across the meadow with Margo. Cleaver and Crista collapsed in the kitchen. Granny Rubin shivered. The evening air was chilly. "Get me my sweater, Sarah," she asked. "It looks like summer is over."

"I'll go down to the diner with Sarah to make supper," Dad said. "What's in the freezer, Nettie?"

"Not much. We could have pastrami and rolls. I froze a cheese cake before we left. And you better feed those two beasts."

There were two notes stuffed under the front door. Mr. Michaels had scribbled, "Welcome back! Good news on the bypass. They canceled it." And a note for me. "I hope you had a good vacation. See you at school. We can stay here. Gilberto Mendoza." I sat for a minute in booth number four and had a good cry, just like Mom. Granny Rubin was right again.

After supper, Dad said he had an announcement. "Mom and I had a great vacation. It did us both a lot of good to be by ourselves again. We spent almost a week at an inn in Switzerland where they take in three or four people who want to learn the inn business."

That feeling in my stomach I had up in Castine returned. I held my breath to see if it would go away. It didn't, so I did the next best thing, which was to take deep—really deep—breaths and hold them. I missed some of what Dad was saying. The next thing I heard was, "And we could take Cleaver, too. I don't know about Crista. What do you think? Wouldn't that be fun, a whole year abroad?"

Granny Rubin didn't say a word. She looked suddenly very sad. Cori's mouth dropped open. While she was trying to figure out what to say, I said, "But we don't have an inn."

Dad smiled. He pulled another surprise out of his hat. "Yes, we do. You've just spent a month in the inn."

Mom spoke for the first time. She didn't sound as decisive as Dad. "Dad and I have been talking about selling the diner and moving up to Castine to open an inn. In a year or two Granny Stuart is going to build a smaller house on the lot next door for herself. She thought you, Mama, might like to share it with her. You could stay with her next year while we're in Europe."

Cori found her breath. "Margo!" she screamed. "Leave Margo? No way, José! No sir, I'll live with the Michaelses. They'll be glad to have me. I can earn my keep or something."

I thought of Rock Hall Academy and how much I disliked it and Muffy Forsythe. And how I was used to living where I lived.

"How do you feel about it, Sarah?" Mom asked.

"I don't know, Mom. I don't think I want to leave the

diner and my friends. You said we all had to agree. I think we all belong here. The Good Luck is a good place to grow up."

"Mama?"

Granny Rubin took a tissue from the pocket of her old sweater. She dabbed at her eyes. "It's hard to leave where you've lived your life, Benedicta. But if it's best for the family, I'll go."

"That's it, Ed," Mom said. "Three to two against. I told you it wouldn't work. If we counted Cleaver, it would be four to two. I don't know about Crista. Tell them about your next idea."

"Well, there's no room in the diner for Nettie and me both. We've discovered that. But there's a lot of room up on the hill, and I thought if we didn't run an inn in Castine, we could have one here in Stanhope. I'll take the inn and Nettie can have the diner, which is hers, anyway. Granny Rubin would have the house and . . ." Dad looked down at Cleaver and Crista, who both raised their heads, looking up for a handout. "We'll give the barn to Crista and Cleaver. How about that?"

The butterflies in my stomach stopped fluttering. I knew we were together for good. I had my wish upon the star. I looked down at the two dogs. It seemed to me that Cleaver nodded his big head once before he let it drop on Crista's back, sighed, and went back to sleep. He was home.